Basic Training

Flying by the Seat of His Pants

P T Saunders

Table of Contents

Basic Training

Flying by the Seat of his Pants

P T Saunders is a veteran of two wars, who also served with the Parachute Regiment and the Special Air Service. Due to his experiences during service, Paul now suffers from Complex PTSD.

Having experienced a particularly traumatic episode in 2011, where he attempted to take his own life on several occasions, medics recommended that he needed to be hospitalised for several weeks, in order to keep himself safe. It was during his stay in hospital that his psychiatrist recommended that Paul write his thoughts down as a form of self-help therapy.

Paul took his advice and wrote his first autobiography "Cupboard Boy". But instead of just locking the book away, Paul decided to self-publish his book. It was the success of this book that inspired Paul to continue writing and exploring different genres.

Chapter One

My Host

I stopped nibbling for a few seconds and took a look around my current location. It was the bedroom of one Ben Baxter, an eighteen-year old zit-riddled and brainless idiot, with a seriously bad attitude to life and absolutely no work ethic whatsoever. Since leaving school nearly two years ago, he'd had several jobs, but, due to his inability to peel himself from his mattress, he had given up on two and been sacked from three. He was what you humans might call "a waste of space".

As my bulbous round eyes scanned the room, I saw that the walls were adorned with pictures of the topless models of the era – 1980 to be precise. There was Linda Lusardi, Samantha Fox and various other topless *Sun* newspaper pinups. All were buxom lasses with big tits. Both Linda and Sam were very popular amongst young boys, and their fathers, too. Directly above Ben's bed on the ceiling was a huge picture of Joan Collins dressed in sexy lingerie, which, I believe, was a screenshot from the film *The Bitch*.

Ben was in his bed ("fleapit" to you and me). He was fast asleep and snoring like a strangulated pig, even though it was already eleven-thirty in the morning.

His room was a bit of a sty, with unwashed clothes, mouldy cups and a few dirty plates of half-eaten midnight snacks tucked under the bed, which were precisely why I had been hanging around for the last few days.

You see, I'm a fly. Not just any old common or garden fly; I'm unique. I can speak English and even use a computer. Which, incidentally, is what I'm writing this, my new "best seller", on. If I were to compare myself to a human form, I would say that I'm a cross between Billy Connolly and Jeremy Clarkson; a kind of sarcastic, Scottish, self-righteous and opinionated bastard, who thinks they're funny but are really just annoying.

Now, I know some of you smartarses out there will say,

'That's impossible, flies only live for a few days and they certainly can't write.'

To you I say, Get over yourself, it's a frigging story, a piece of fiction. Stop moaning and either carry on reading or get your money back. Life is too short.

As I was saying, I've been a guest of Ben's for a couple of days now, and not because I like him. No, it's because I love the fact that, on a nightly basis, he collapses onto his bed half-cut and with a snack of some sort or another, which he hardly ever eats.

For me, it's a bit like a kind of room-service. So, I thought I'd hang around for a while.

I had just started on last night's half-eaten cheese and pickle sandwich, when Ben's mother, June, came bursting into the room with all the subtleness of an elephant running through a crockery shop; she was obviously on a mission.

'Ben…" she said, in a slightly louder voice than a whisper. 'Ben…?' A bit louder this time. Getting no response, she bellowed 'Ben!' a few more times before Ben finally woke up and responded.

'What do you bloody want?' he mumbled from underneath the covers.

'For a start, I want you to get your lazy arse out of that bed before midday for once in your life. You lazy little shit!' screeched his mother. And you need to sign on, too, you know they'll stop your benefits if you miss your signing time,' she added as she exited Ben's room, slamming the door shut and nearly taking it off its hinges.

Reminder to oneself; Don't annoy her, I thought as I carried on chomping away.

Ben rolled over onto his back and, like most other oversexed and unlucky in love eighteen-year olds, found he had woken up with a woody (a hard-on). He looked up at the poster of Joan and started to tug on his erect member. Just as he was rather quickly getting to the point of no return, the door to his bedroom burst open once more.

'And you've…' his mother was rendered temporarily speechless and rooted to the spot by the sight of her son tugging on his rather large member. '…got a letter from the army. You filthy, little bugger,' she added, exiting the room rather more quickly than she had entered.

Ben, undeterred by the embarrassing moment, continued to finish the job off into his sock. *Grubby human.* He then managed to extract himself from the pit he called his bed. After waiting for a few seconds and making sure his penis was once again flaccid, he made his way toward the kitchen.

I, of course, had no intention of missing the conversation that was about to take place. *This should be interesting,* I thought as I followed Ben into the kitchen – being careful to avoid the sticky fly strip that dangled from the ceiling.

'Is there any breakfast going?' Ben asked, yawning and scratching his head with one hand, while re-arranging his man-tackle with the other.

'No, there bloody well isn't, you lazy bugger. Oh, and I hope you used tissue and not your bloody sock like you usually do, you dirty so and so,' she scolded.

'Mum, do you have to?' Ben moaned as he cupped his hungover head in his hands.

'Here, this came for you, it's from the army,' his mother said as she handed him a brown envelope.

Ben took the letter and threw it on top of the microwave.

'Don't you want to open that; it might be important?' asked Ben's mum, dying to know what was in it.

'No, but you can if you like,' Ben said as he searched the fridge for some milk.

Thinking it might be good news, i.e. the army was going to give her a break from her son's lazy ways, June grabbed the letter and tore it open. As she read the contents, I noticed a broad smile appear on her face.

'Yes! Yes! And yes!' she screamed excitedly in her head as she read the following:

"I am pleased to tell you that you have been selected to attend the Army Selection Centre, Sutton Coalfield." She read on.

"Enclosed is a Rail Travel Warrant; please attend on Wednesday the 12th of May."

That's tomorrow, she thought.

'It says you've been selected to go to Sutton Coalfield tomorrow,' she informed her son, who, on hearing the news, nearly choked on his dry corn flakes.

'I can't go tomorrow; it's too short notice,' Ben winged it.

'You're bloody going and that's it, or you can bloody well sling your hook, you lazy good for sod all!' shouted his mother.

Nice mother-son relationship, I thought to myself as I regurgitated on Ben's cornflakes.

'I'll need some money if I'm going,' muttered Ben.

'I can give you a tenner for the journey,' replied his mum. *She'll obviously do anything to get rid of him,* I thought.

A few seconds later, another thought came bouncing into my head; *Ben (El Slobbo) going through basic army training? Now, this is something I have to see.* Then I had the worst idea of my entire life: I decided that I would follow him on his pointless journey. After all, what could go wrong?

Chapter Two

The Train

The following day, at eight in the morning, Ben's mum once again came bursting into his bedroom.

'Ben, Ben, get up! You need to get packed and down to the station in an hour,' she said as she shook him awake.

'Muuum, leave me alone,' Ben mumbled from beneath the covers.

'No, I will not leave you alone until you're out of bed and in that bathroom,' she shouted, shaking him once more for good measure.

'Alright, alright,' said Ben as he threw the sheets back and showed himself once again to be sporting a woody – embarrassing his mother once again.

After showering and eating the "special going-away breakfast" his mother had prepared for him, Ben packed an overnight bag and set off on his journey of discovery, while I hitched a ride on his back. After all, why fly and waste energy when you can get a lift?

We arrived at Crewe Station with only minutes to spare before our train was due to depart. We had made it just in time!

As Ben flopped into his seat, he nearly crushed me but actually succeeded in squashing the fly who had been sitting next to me on his back and which was now a stain on Ben's jacket. I decided to take my revenge by continuing to fly in and out of Ben's ear, making him slap himself a few times while trying to swat me. He didn't manage to get me, of course; that would have made this book a rapid read.

About an hour into our two-hour journey, I began to get a bit peckish. So, as all flies do, I decided to take a tour of the surroundings, looking out for some grotty little kid with a bag of crisps or a little old granny eating a crumbly cheese sandwich.

Having had no luck, I was hungrily making my way back to our seat, when I saw Ben heading for the buffet car.

Hoping he would buy one of the lovely cheese and pickle sandwiches I'd seen earlier, I tagged along. And, as luck would have it, he did indeed buy the very same sandwich. *Yummy,* I thought, as we made our way back to Ben's seat.

When we arrived, there was another young, spotty-faced teen sitting in the seat opposite Ben's.

After a few silent, sizing-up moments, they greeted one and other:

'Hi, I'm Ben.'

'Fred,' replied the other fellow.

They very quickly entered into conversation, and it didn't take them long to realise they were both going to the same place for the same reason.

Fred, a spotty-faced, stick-thin lad was from Liverpool. He was your typical Scouser, cocky and full of bullshit. According to him, he'd done everything, seen everything and had multiple T-shirts to prove it. He was one of nine siblings, five of whom were in jail for various criminal offences, another was serving time in the military "glass house" and the other two were not old enough to have committed any offences – yet. He was totally full of shit. And, due to his lack of school attendance, he was also as thick as shit.

Great, I now have two dickheads to follow, I thought.

Then Ben did something that really pissed me off! He offered his new bessie-mate half his cheese sandwich. Worse still, the cheeky scouse git took it!

That meant no cheese sandwich for me. You see, it's normal for someone to leave half the sandwich on the table while eating the other half, allowing me and any other flies prone to a nibble the opportunity to dive in and fill our boots.

Now that both halves of the sandwich were in each of their grubby hands, I had no chance.

Pissed off or what?

Chapter Three

All Aboard the Welcome Coach

We arrived at Birmingham New Street at precisely ten-thirty that morning and disembarked. As we did so, Ben noticed an army sergeant standing on the platform.

Sergeant Fisher was his name; a tall but fat man, who obviously knew of a good pie shop or two. He had a dark-brown lampshade moustache that reminded me of a caterpillar. He probably thought that the moustache made him look more macho. It didn't, at least, not according to one of the other two sergeants, who were standing at the doors of another army coach and one of whom was going to be Fisher's replacement. Apparently, Fisher had served in the Welsh Guards for the last twenty-one years and was in his final year of service. Due to his extreme lack of fitness, he was deemed superfluous to requirements by his own regiment and had been duly dumped on the selection centre.

He had never been to war, nor had he been on a tour of Northern Ireland. The only fighting he had seen was when his two-ton-Tessie of a wife, known as "Sumo-Sally", saved him from getting a kicking by single-handily taking out four paratroopers, who were about to beat the shit out of him for being a "Hat" (non-paratrooper) and daring to walk into the Pegasus pub, where she was a barmaid.

So, relieved at being saved from the beating of his life, he accepted her invitation to move on to another pub with her. There he got so drunk that he slept with her and impregnated her with their first child. Six months later, she made him marry her.

Over nineteen years of marriage, they went on to have a further seven children. All girls. All fat bitches. None of whom liked or respected him. He often thought about leaving the fat cows but didn't dare. Sally would probably kill him.

We all made our way to the sour-faced sergeant, and Ben asked if he was here to collect them.

The sergeant stared at them for several seconds before responding – an obvious attempt to try to intimidate the lads. It didn't work, though; I heard one of the other lads muttering "fucking knob-jockey".

'If you're going to Sutton, I sure am, sir; just step through the door over there and get onboard the green army coach,' replied the sergeant very politely, wearing a stupid plastic smile on his face.

'He seems nice enough,' said Fred to Ben.

Sucker! Even I knew that was an act to fool them into a false sense of security. Dumb Scouse git!

Anyway, we made our way to the green coach and boarded.

As Ben and Fred took their seats, I was once again nearly flattened. This time by zit-faced Fred. Normally, I would have had a go at him, but by then I was too tired and starving hungry to care.

Twenty minutes later, when the sergeant boarded, the bus was full of similar, smelly, zit-faced teens.

'Right gentlemen, my name is Sergeant Fisher, spelled B-A-R-S-T-A-R-D, and you are now in the army and, as such, you are my new bitches. If I say jump, you ask how high. If I say get down, you ask how low.'

Stupid dumb fuck; even I know that's not how you spell "bastard", and I'm a bloody fly. It's official, the army only hires the brainless and the damaged!

'Do you understand me?' asked the sergeant.
A few of the kids murmured a limp 'Yes, Sergeant.'

'I'm sorry, I didn't quite fucking hear you. Do you understand?' the sergeant screamed in a kind of pantomime way, holding his hand to his ear.

The whole coach responded this time.

'Yes, Sergeant," they screamed at the tops of their voices.

'That's better. Now, sit back and zip this (he drew his finger along his lips), relax and enjoy the ride.'

The forty-minute journey seemed more like four hours as the recruits sat in silence, probably contemplating what was in store for them. Some of them were probably wishing they had never taken the Queen's shilling.

Chapter Four

Army Selection Centre

When our coach arrived at the selection centre at about midday, it was absolutely peeing it down. As the coach passed through the red and white vehicular barrier, I could see groups of young men all wearing red V-necked T-shirts and green trousers. Some groups were marching, another group was doing push-ups and others were running. They were all piss-wet through. Each group also had their very own corporal or sergeant, who was bellowing insults and orders at them.

By the time the coach came to a halt, I was so hungry I could have eaten a horse. Thanks to greedy bastard Fred, I never did get to eat any of Ben's cheese and pickle sandwiches. I was now really looking forward to downing some army scran. However, my belly had to wait another hour or so, while Ben and his fellow idiots were frogmarched over to the quartermaster's stores, where they were issued (thrown) their bedding, boots, a red V-necked PT shirt, a pair of khaki trousers and a plastic-covered green mattress.

Once all the recruits had been issued with their kit, they were again frogmarched to the accommodation block – their home for the next twenty-four hours.

By the time they arrived at the block, half of them had dropped most of their kit, leaving a trail of boots, sheets and uniform behind them. Those that didn't have their full complement of issued equipment were told to stand to one side, while the recruits, all three of them, with all their kit were sent to their rooms. The rest were told to assume the press-up position and give the sergeant twenty push-ups. After which, they were all told to gather up their now soaking wet kit and form up outside the quartermaster's stores. From there, they were again frogmarched back to the accommodation block. This sequence of events happened a total of seven times, until every man had made it back to the block with a full complement of kit. I bet you can guess who the last man to enter the building was.

By the time Ben and Fred had eventually got into the block, there were only two bed spaces available. Disappointingly for me, they were in the same room. *Great, now I'm stuck with stupid Scouse,* I thought to myself.

The rooms had ten bed spaces, each comprising a bed and a green metal locker. There was an iron hanging on one of the walls, and next to it was a single ironing board. In the far corner of the room stood what looked like a mop, but was rectangular in shape and made of cast iron and heavy as hell. It was the dreaded floor buffer. It may have been archaic, but it had been used to buff the wooden floor to with an inch of its life. It shone like plate glass, and the air in the room was thick with the smell of waxy polish.

The guys had just about stowed their gear away when they heard the donkey-bellow once more.

'Fall in outside, the last one on parade gets my boot up their arse.'

With none of them wanting to be the last one on parade and feel the sergeant's size eleven boot, the whole squad legged it, causing a mini-stampede. Once formed up outside, the recruits were marched over to the cookhouse.

Chapter Five

As Hungry as a Horse

It took forever to get to the cookhouse but not because it was miles away. The problem was that the sergeant kept making them do press-ups every hundred yards for talking in the ranks. As you can probably guess, Ben and Fred were two of those caught chatting.

I'm so hungry, I could eat a horse, I thought to myself as the recruits were finally allowed to enter the cookhouse. The boys, Ben and his cronies, all formed a queue. I, though, being a fly just dived straight in there. There was row upon row of goodies on offer, from quiche, fried chicken, curry and there was even a salad bar — my favourite place; a fly can linger amongst the coleslaw and cold pasta for ages without being disturbed. Whereas the hot plate was a totally different kettle of fish. A hot plate is a fly's worst nightmare. If you're not being swatted by one of the serving chefs, you get your ass burnt from the hot lights. Give me a deserted salad bar any day of the week.

As I flew past the hot plates on the way to the salad bar, I noticed that quite a few of my fellow flies had been slaughtered and were now either lying face up in the food or were hot and crispy on the hotplate edges. There were so many of them, it nearly put me off my lunch. It didn't, though. I was just watching one of my comrades flapping its wing desperately in a bid to free itself from a bowl of chili, when I felt the gust of air which preceded the swinging spatula that was meant for my head. I made a rapid retreat. In fact, I flew out of there so fast that I flew smack bang into the glass counter cover. Ouch!

Now very pissed off and with a headache to boot, I decided to take revenge by going from dish to dish and defecating several times on every single meal. Fact: **Flies defecate every time they land**. After this, I got the would-be killer slop-jockey to slap himself across the head a few times by buzzing around and landing on his hairy ears.

Within ten minutes of the lads arriving at the cookhouse, the foul-mouthed Sergeant Donkey popped his ugly head around the cookhouse door and bellowed, 'Time's up, get your arses on parade!'

Most of the lads hadn't even been served, and those that had simply stuffed whatever they could into their mouths as they legged it to the door.

Once again, the lads fell over each other in an effort not to be the last out.

I was so busy completing my sabotage mission that, by the time I went to join them, the door to the cookhouse was well and truly shut. Therefore, I had to make my exit via a window in the kitchen.

As I flew through the kitchen, I noticed the very familiar blueish lights of Eazyzap UV fly killers hanging around the walls.

Unfortunately, several dozen of my colleagues who hadn't noticed them in time were now lying lifeless on the floor below.

Murderous bastards!

As I exited through the rear via an open window, I heard the familiar **buzz-splat!** sound of yet another of my not-so-observant comrades connecting with an Eazyzap.

Chapter Six
B-Billy the K-Kid

By the time I arrived at the front of the cookhouse, all the recruits were once again being marched to where … I didn't have a clue. I caught up with them just as they were finishing up yet another set of press-ups, before being lined up outside the barber's shop.

The sergeant chose ten of the recruits to enter the shop and ordered the rest to wait outside and go in as the others came out. That was a bit of a bummer, as it was just starting to rain again. Unluckily for Ben and Fred, they were not amongst the first ten victims. They were actually at the back of the queue.

I suppose I should have stayed outside with them. But, to be honest, I hate the rain; every drop that connects feels like someone is dropping a sack of spuds on my head. So, I ditched the bitches and entered with the first ten recruits.

Once inside, I saw that the shop had two cutting stations and eight waiting seats along the opposite wall. The floor around the two cutting stations was covered in a layer at least four inches thick of multi-coloured hair of varying lengths. This was the hair of the previously butchered bunch of recruits.

Just above the mirrors on the workstation wall, there was a row of photo frames with styles numbered one to ten. The word was spelled "stile". *Dumb fucks.* Each frame had the same hairstyle

— a number-two crew cut. Below a sign read "You Choose". *Very fucking funny,* I thought to myself as I inspected the rest of the shop.

On the back wall, which housed a door marked "Private", were a few posters of the now very familiar topless Sam Fox and Linda Lusardi. Pinned to the ceiling at both ends of the room were more fly terminators. This time they were in the form of flycatcher strips. These are particularly nasty pieces of kit. If a fly lands on one, they end up being stuck there and death is cruelly slow.

It's funny how humankind spends millions of pounds developing various devices whose sole purpose is to torture and kill flies. Really, are we that annoying?

The barbers were both civilians in their sixties. Tom and Billy were identical twins, one of whom, Billy, had a very bad stammer. Unfortunately, he was also the most talkative of the two.

'N-n-n-next v-v-v-victim,' said Billy, smiling and flashing his fag stained teeth as he holstered his clippers like a geriatric John Wayne. The lads laughed hysterically. One of them even fell off his chair, which caused even more hysterics.

The humourless and disapproving look on Billy's face quickly turned the laughter to silent sniggers every time he spoke.

Through the reflection in the wall-mirror, I could see him still glaring at the waiting clients. To say that he wasn't happy was a definite understatement!

I was having a pretty bad time, too. Virtually everyone in the shop had tried to swat me at least twice whenever I landed to take a break from flying. So, I decided that the next time the door opened, I would make a run for it and see some more of the selection centre.

It wasn't long before I was free and noticed that Ben and Fred were still toward the back of the queue. That gave me at least an hour to explore.

As I flew around, I could see that the place was vast. There were groups of troops marching (trying to march) on the square. There was another group running, shouldering what seemed to be a telegraph pole. It wasn't clear why. A third group was clambering over an assault course.

The next building I came across was the guardroom, which was at the entrance to the barracks. There, I saw some poor kid running around in circles carrying a highly-polished, chrome-coloured dustbin above his head. The poor kid looked half dead.

I wonder what he's been up to deserve his personalised beasting? It's at times like these that I'm glad to be a mere fly on the wall. I made my way back to the barbershop via the NAAFI cake counter.

I arrived back at the barber's just in time to enter the shop with Ben, Fred and another of Ben's new BFF's, Teddy Edwards.

Teddy was from Bexhill-on-Sea, which is on the east coast of Sussex. Being an only child of a couple of head teachers, he was well educated and wanted for nothing. Being from a small village, he was not very streetwise and was, therefore, quite vulnerable.

Again, after ten minutes or so, Billy the barber came out with 'N-n-next V-v-victim,' as he, once again, comically tried to holster his clippers and missed, sending the clippers crashing to the floor. This had the lads in stitches again. As you might expect, Ben had to go a step further, saying, 'Oo-oh dd-d-dear, I m-m-missed a-a-again.' I was expecting Billy the barber to absolutely go ape. He didn't; he just glared at El Slobbo as he picked up his clippers and carried on. The mood in the shop was now so tense that you could have cut the atmosphere with a knife.

Unfortunately for Ben, he was one of the last two customers of the day. So, when Billy the barber beckoned him to his chair with a swoop of his hand and a smile on his face that the Cheshire Cat would have been envious of, both Ben and I knew that he had drawn the short straw.

Excited at the thought that Ben was about to get some comeuppance, I landed myself a front-row seat on the edge of the mirror.

Billy the barber, still staring at Ben, slowly unholstered his clippers, paused for a few seconds, then, as if hitting the trip-switch on a bomb, flicked the switch to "on", bringing the clippers roaring back to life.

He smiled at Ben once more. It was supposed to be tense, like a gunfight at the O.K. Corral. Instead, it was more like a comedy sketch as Billy dramatically flipped off the number-two cutting guide, taking the cutting length to one, before beginning to scalp the right side of Ben's head, lopping off great chunks of his shoulder-length hair. All that was missing was the soundtrack to *The Good, the Bad, and the Ugly*. Only in this case, it was more like the stupid, the fat and the f-ugly.

Billy's smile stretched from ear to ear as he carefully and purposely scalped the whole of the right side of Ben's head. Then, suddenly, Billy whipped off the protective gown that protected El Slobbo's clothes.

'Right, it's f-f-five o-o-o'clock. We close at f-f-five, so you can f-f-fuck off until tomorrow, you little sh-shit,' he announced as he pointed to the door.

Ben was about to protest when the door to the shop was flung open. It was the sergeant. 'Right everyone, out and on parade,' he bellowed.

'But…' Ben tried to protest.

'Out!' bellowed the sergeant once more.

Not wanting to get on the wrong side of the giant of a sergeant, both Ben and Fred flew out of their chairs and were outside in a flash. Luckily for Fred, Tom had finished his haircut.

Outside, all the recruits were ordered to line up in single file. The sergeant then walked along the line and inspected each of the recruits' haircuts. When he reached Ben, he could hardly contain his laughter.

'Have you been taking the piss out of our B-B-Billy by any chance?' he asked, before bursting into laughter. Which, in turn, sent the rest of the recruits into hysterics.

At this point, I almost felt I should feel a little sorry for Ben. I didn't, though; I still hadn't forgiven him for the cheese and pickle sandwich incident.

The recruits were then reformed into three ranks and were once again frogmarched back to their accommodation block.

Chapter Seven
Over the Fence

Once back at the accommodation, Sergeant Donkey dismissed them:

'Right you bunch of bloody blundering baboons, the rest of the day is yours to do with as you will. However, you are to remain in the camp. You are not permitted in the NAFFI bar. Teatime is from six to six-thirty. Any questions?'

There was a short pause before Ben apprehensively raised his right hand.

'Yes, Haircut, what is it?'

'What time are you picking us up tomorrow morning, Sarge?'

'Sarge? Did you just call me sarge, Haircut? In the army, dickhead, there are only two kinds of sarge; sausarge, as in the meaty little things you have with your breakfast, and massarge. Are you calling me a sausage, Haircut? Or are you hoping for a fucking oily rubdown? Well, Haircut, which is it?'

'Neither, Sergeant,' replied the now red-faced and half-bald Ben.

'As to what time "I'll be picking you up", I'm also not a fucking kerb crawler. I don't go around picking little shits like you up for a good old bumming,' said the sergeant, sending the whole squad into hysterics all over again.

Once calm amongst the ranks was restored, the sergeant made them all do a further twenty push-ups. He then informed them that they should be on parade at 08.00 hrs before dismissing them.

I have decided that from this point on, Ben will be known as **Haircut**.

Once the lads were in their rooms and they had all introduced themselves, talk soon turned to jumping the fence and going out for a few beers. One of the lads, Jimmy James, was from the local area and promised to show the lads a good night out if they took him with them.

'I can't go out looking like this,' moaned Haircut, pointing to his head. 'I'll be a fucking laughingstock.'

'Anyone got a pair of scissors?' asked Fred. His request was met with a chorus of "no's".

Fred thought about how he might help his new BFF out… 'I know, we can use one of my razor blades. Or you could just wear a hat.'

'No hat,' said Haircut, looking and seeing everyone shake their heads.

'Blade it is, then,' said Fred as he rummaged through his holdall looking for his shaving kit.

Twenty or so minutes later, Haircut was looking at his reflection in his locker door mirror. He was now almost completely bald, and his head was covered in a multitude of razor bites.

Haircut now looks even more of a twat than before the makeover! I thought, surveying Fred's handy work.

Undeterred by the unsightly look of his head, Haircut, Fred, Jimmy, Teddy Edwards and two of the other lads, Sid and Pizza-Face Pete, jumped the fence just after dinner. Not wishing to miss out on a bit of fun, I tagged along, too. After all, it would be difficult for me to write this next chapter without being there.

Chapter Eight
The Beast of Birmingham

It took about forty minutes or so before we reached the first pub. The Cock Inn was a grubby back-street boozer, full of beer-swilling Irish navvies. The air inside stank of cigarettes and weed, and the carpets were so mucky that most people wiped their feet on the way out.

Having visited the barbers earlier and now modelling the distinctive military crew cut, the boys started to be a little concerned about being in the presence of so many micks.

'For all we know, some of them might even be IRA sympathisers,' I heard one member of the group say, before they hastily drank up and moved on to the next pub.

'I want to go somewhere with music and women,' demanded Pizza-Face.

'I know exactly the place, then. And my mate's dad is a bouncer on the door, so we'll get in for free, too. Mind you, the drinks are dearer,' replied Jimmy.

'I don't care, so long as there are women and lots of them,' responded Pizza-Face.

'It's a titty bar, so there's bound to be,' said Jimmy, cupping his man boobs to emphasize the point.

Ten minutes later we arrived at the bar – which, funnily enough, was called the Titty Bar.

Very fucking original, I thought as I hitched a ride in on the back of Haircut's coat.

The place was dark and very poorly lit, probably to soften the looks of some of the most unattractive hostesses. They were, unfortunately, wearing thong-bikinis. One of them had a tattoo on the small of her back which read "Free Parking", below which was an arrow pointing to her ass. *Classy.* It was obvious to me that the bosses saved the good-looking girls for the busier weekends; this lot were definitely the runts of the hostess litter.

The lads approached the bar to order some drinks.

'Sorry, gentlemen, it's hostess service only. Please take a seat and one of our hostesses will come and take your orders,' said the girl behind the bar, whose face was covered in enough makeup to sink a battleship. She had huge tits, too, which almost fell out of her skimpy top as she waved the boys away with a dramatic and slightly aggressive hand gesture.

Stuck-up slapper, I thought to myself as I followed the boys to a booth-like seating area.

A few seconds later, we were surrounded by five bikini-clad slappers.

'Hi, boys, do you fancy some company?' asked the tall, flat-chested blonde.

'Y-yes,' said Teddy, who had been sporting a semi ever since he'd walked through the door. *Obviously a virgin.*

The four girls took seats next to each of the guys, whilst the fifth took the drinks order.

'Are you buying the girls one, too?' she asked.

The lads looked at each other and nodded in agreement.

'Of course,' said Haircut, speaking on behalf of the group.

Now, I know I'm only a common or garden fly, but even I knew that offering to buy these cock teasers a drink was going to be a costly mistake. But hey, it's their money!

After about twenty minutes, Haircut and Fred, who were not feeling the love, suggested that the group move on to a disco and asked one of the lasses for the bill. On hearing Haircut's request, all the girls rapidly dispersed to other tables. They didn't even say "thanks" or "goodbye".

Two minutes later, the bill arrived.

'There you go, sir,' said the slapper from behind the bar, smiling like the Cheshire Cat.

Ben took the bill and nearly fell through the floor as he read the list of charges.

Larger Pint	X 5	£30.00
Champagne	X 5	£75.00
Hostess service charge X 4		£100.00
Service charge @ 15%		£30.75
Total		**£235.75**

Thank you for your custom.

'Holy fucking shit, it can't be that much,' said Haircut as he showed the rest of the group the bill, with each in turn gasping at the extortionate amount, before protesting that they didn't have the money to pay it and, even if they had, they wouldn't pay it.

After a few long silent moments of the barmaid staring at them, it was decided that they would refuse to pay for the champagne and the hostess charge. They also nominated Jimmy as the eldest and the one who had brought them here to break the news to the bitch at the bar.

A minute or so after Jimmy had approached the bar, two black bouncers, both built like proverbial brick shithouses, and I joined Jimmy at the bar. They chatted for a while. Actually, the bouncers threatened to break Jimmy's legs if he didn't pay up, and, eventually, the bar slag produced a card machine and Jimmy handed over a card.

'That will be two-hundred and forty-one pounds and fifty pence,' said the smug cow.

'It says two-hundred and thirty pounds on the bill,' protested Jimmy.

'There's a five per cent credit card charge,' replied the barmaid, with a look on her face that seemed to ask if Jimmy was stupid or something.

Eventually, Jimmy and I joined the rest of the group and we left.

Outside, Jimmy recounted the conversation that took place with the bouncers.

'They said that if we didn't pay, we would all end up visiting A&E, and, as the spokesman, I would be the first to get my legs broken. So, I paid the bill with my credit card. Now you all owe me forty-one quid each.'

They all promised to send Jimmy the money as soon as they were paid. Jimmy, being a dumb sucker, accepted their word.

After such a close call, the lads decided that they should call it a night. However, on the way back to the barracks they came across the a pub called the Black Pig, which just so happened to be rocking and full of skirts of varying sizes and ages. After checking what money they had left between them, it was decided that they would have one last drink or two, and so they entered the bar.

The place was jam-packed, mostly with women.

'This is more like it. Look at the amount of fanny in here,' said Teddy, whose eyes and pants were bulging at the sight of some scantily-clad lasses obviously on a hen do. *He's so obviously a virgin that he'll be known from now on as "Virgin",* I thought to myself as I dived over to a table laid out with a buffet.

It was great; I managed to get me some cheese and pickle sandwich and a bit of quiche, without anyone trying to assassinate me.

Once I had refuelled, I re-joined Haircut and his mates. They were standing with their backs to the bar staring at a group of right bitches. However, as with all groups of women found in bars, there are always the odd ugly and one or two fat ones.

'Do you reckon she's going commando?' Haircut asked the group, pointing at a tall, quite good-looking lass wearing a belt for a skirt.

'Commando. What's commando?' Asked Virgin. The rest of the group laughed out loud.

'Going commando is when a chick doesn't wear any knickers, you virgin,' explained Jimmy.

'Oh, I see,' replied Virgin, looking a little embarrassed.

'Not that any of us will ever get the chance to find out. She's well out of our league,' said Sid.

You lot might not be able to confirm or otherwise, but I'm a fly; I can go anywhere; So, with that in mind, I decided to check it out on the boys' behalf.

I took a peek at the lass with a belt for a skirt first. It only took a short flight to discover that she was indeed going commando. *Tart,* I thought to myself, surveying the whole hen pack one by one. And the results were ... eight out of ten hens were going commando. The other two, a couple of fat lasses, whose privates resembled parts of the Amazonian jungle, weren't holding out for a quick grope any time soon!

Eventually, Jimmy and Haircut summoned up the balls to approach the lasses and ask if they and their friends might join them. Jenny, one of the fat birds, spoke for the girls.

'You and your mates can buy us a drink if you like,' she said, whilst giving Haircut a wanton stare.

Poor bugger, I thought as I watched Haircut gulp in fear at the thought of having to bonk Jumbo Jenny.

Jimmy waived the rest of the lads over to join them. He then informed the girls that they were all pretty much broke. He cited what had happened in the club earlier as his excuse for not being able to get the drinks in.

'Shouldn't go to titty bars, they're immoral,' stated one of the girls.

'Trust me, we won't be going to another one any time soon,' said Jimmy, still smarting at his credit card getting a hammering.

Feeling a little sorry for Haircut and clearly desperate for a shag, Jumbo Jenny wrapped her arms around him.

'It's okay, darlin', I'll look after you,' she said, whilst slapping a kiss on his cheek and giving him a "your luck's in" smile as she dragged him to the bar.

Poor sod, I thought as I continued my commando survey, while taking the odd break to snack on the various bits of leftover bar snacks adorning a few of the tables.

By the time I had re-united with the group, they had all but one (Virgin) copped off with one of the lasses. They were all snogging the faces off each other, including Haircut and Jumbo Jenny. *She must have doped him or something.*

At midnight, having exhausted their joint funds, all but two of the couples parted ways. Jumbo Jenny had somehow convinced the now pissed Haircut to go back to hers for "a coffee". *Now, this I can't miss,* I thought, promptly hitching a ride Jumbo's pink Alice band.

Chapter Nine

Time to Jump

The following morning, Haircut opened his eyes very slowly. He winced as the morning's bright sunlight stung the back of his eyes.

Serves you right sucker,' I thought as I stretched out my wings.

He glanced over to his right and was met by the sight of the top of Jumbo's head. 'Shit,' he said, accidentally out loud. He seemed to be genuinely shocked to find himself lying next to Jumbo, who was away with the fairies and snoring like a pig. Haircut apprehensively lifted the covers. 'Bollocks,' he said, finding himself to be stark bollock naked.

I could tell from the look of dread on his face that he had little or no recollection of the previous evening's events. I, on the other hand, being a teetotaller, had been scarred for life at what I had seen them getting up to!

I won't go into too much detail, but I bet he has a sore arse this morning. She was an animal!

Haircut tried to slowly extract himself and his early morning woody from the fleapit of a bed without disturbing the sleeping Jumbo. He nearly managed it, too. However, just then the clock struck seven-thirty and the alarm sounded, "Cock-a-doodle-doo!"

In a panic, Haircut quickly located the clock and hit the snooze button. It was too late, though.

'Hiya, lover,' said the now wide-awake Jumbo as she grabbed his semi-erect member.

'Get off me, woman, I'm going to be late getting back to the camp,' protested Haircut as he attempted to get dressed.

"You don't have to worry about being late. You're already on camp.'

Haircut froze to the spot. 'What?' He paused for a moment whilst the news sunk in, then pulled back the curtains to reveal the sight of the parade ground a few hundred feet away.

He turned to Jumbo. 'I don't get it.' He said, with a look of complete dumbness on his face.

'My dad is in the army, and he's based here,' explained Jumbo, attempting once again to get a rise out of his penis.

'Get the fuck off me,' said Haircut, thinking for a few seconds. 'Please tell me his name isn't Sergeant Fisher.'

'Actually, it is. And he's probably in the kitchen as we speak,' growled the rejected Jumbo before flopping back on the bed.

Oh shit, it gets better by the minute,' I thought to myself.

'Holy shit! I need to get out of here. Like yesterday. What's the best way of avoiding your dad?' asked Haircut.

A smug smile grew on Jumbo's face as she turned her head slowly toward the bedroom window.

'Oh, bollocks,' said Haircut as he surveyed the drop before scrambling through the window, nearly breaking his neck as he landed in the flower bed below. I quickly followed on behind.

Chapter Ten

Baggy Trousers

We eventually made it back to the accommodation with fifteen minutes spare before the lads were due on parade.

'You're cutting it a bit fine; you've only got ten minutes,' Virgin said, whilst pointing at his rather bulky and gay-looking Casio c80 digital watch.

'It'll only take a minute or … shit, the fucking bastards!' Haircut said out loud as he realised that he'd been issued with a pair of fatigue trousers about six times his size. They were so big that they could have camouflaged a bloody Chieftain tank!

The rest of the room fell about in stitches as they saw Haircut's predicament. I, too, nearly pissed myself with laughter. He looked a right twat!

'Has anyone got a belt?' Haircut asked, his eyes scanning the room's occupants. Each one shook their heads.

'What about this?' called out Virgin, extracting a length of cord from a pair of striped PJ bottoms.

The room was once again filled with laughter at the realisation that an eighteen-year-old and potential killer was still wearing PJ's.

'Thanks, that will have to do for now,' said Haircut, taking the cord and threading it through his trouser belt hoops.

A few minutes later, the group of recruits was once again lined up in three rows outside the accommodation block as Sergeant Fisher marched across the parade square towards them.

'Good morning, you bunch of reprobates,' Fisher said, grinning from ear to ear.

He must have got some last night. Or, maybe he managed to avoid having to have sex with Sumo Sally and thus negated the chance of impregnating her with another baby girl. Or perhaps the smile on his face was down to the fact that he knew he would be having some fun at the expense of the one with the baggy trousers.

He walked along each of the aisles, stopping occasionally to insult the odd recruit. Eventually, he was standing in front of Haircut, his smile growing even wider.

'Morning, Haircut, how are you on this fine and sunny morning? I see you drew the short straw once again,' Fisher said, looking down at Haircut's trousers.

'Yes, Sergeant,' bellowed Haircut in reply.

'Tell me, Haircut, is that piece of rope holding your trousers up army issue?'

'No, Sergeant.'

'Well, get the fucking thing off, man. You can't go mixing civilian clothing with a military uniform.'

'But…' Haircut attempted to plead his case, but Fisher had already moved on to his next victim.

After the mini-inspection, Fisher attempted to get them to march onto the parade ground.

Once on the parade ground, he decided to have a little fun with them. He made them line up in single file and ordered them to jog around the outer perimeter of the parade ground. He also instructed them that on the command "jump", they would have to do a star-jump, which, for clarification, he demonstrated several times.

Now, this should be interesting, I thought to myself, as the only thing now keeping Haircut's trousers up were the dangly things on the end of his arms.

'Haircut, since you were the only one who hasn't yet completed a star-jump, you can go first,' said the sergeant as he pointed to the opposite corner of the parade square. Haircut set off jogging, and within forty or so paces came the first 'jump' command. Needless to say, as Haircut's arms went out to the side, his trousers headed south, exposing his Superman logo-emblazoned underpants.

This sent the rest of the squad into hysterics every time Haircut jumped.

I actually felt sorry for Haircut. And I was feeling a little protective of him, too. So, I decided to give Fisher a little reminder of how annoying my species can be. I flew into various orifices, his right and left nostrils, and his ears, too. This caused him to slap himself about his head several times. He looked as though he was having a fit. Now the squad was laughing at him as he danced like a monkey on coke, trying to avoid my irritating jabs and fly-passes.

Eventually, Haircut was allowed to re-join the rest of the squad. As he lined up, a figure approached from behind the sergeant. It was Jumbo Jenny and, to make matters worse for

Haircut, she was dressed in school uniform. As she passed behind the sergeant, her dad, she blew Haircut a kiss.

'Paedophile,' I heard one of the other lads mutter as she did so.

It just isn't your day, I thought to myself. Sergeant Fisher, now fully recovered from my little bit of fun, had regained his composure and attempted to get the squad marching toward the gym, where the lads would undergo a medical check-up before taking a Basic Fitness Test (BFT).

Chapter Eleven
Is That It?

Once in the gymnasium, the boys were ordered to strip to their socks and shreddies (underpants) and told to line up before a very attractive and sexy looking female doctor, who didn't have a problem with exposing rather a lot of her ample breasts, and who appeared from behind a green portable screen.

Haircut, being the knob he is, gave out a wolf whistle. This didn't go unnoticed by either the doctor or Sergeant Fisher, who shot Haircut an evil look.

This should be interesting, I thought as I watched a bulge slowly appear in Virgin's Y-fronts.

'Right, you lot, drop 'em,' yelled Fisher.

They all simultaneously dropped their draws and, as expected, Virgin's knob, now full of the red stuff, was trying to stand to attention. The rest of the lads started to giggle at the sight of Virgin trying to hide his rather large semi-erect penis. Truth be told, they were probably all jealous of the size of his beast of manhood.

Eventually, big tits made her way along the line of naked recruits, grabbing their balls and asking them to cough. When she got to Haircut, she took a step back and rubbed her chin as she studied Haircut's rather limp and average-sized penis.

'Is that it? Is that actually a penis, Sergeant?' she asked as she stepped forward and gave Haircut's balls a tight squeeze. 'Cough,' she said, with an evil but rather sexy smile on her face.

'You're right, ma'am, it's not much of one. I think Haircut here should be applying to join the WRAC's,' (Women's Royal Army Corps) replied the sergeant, wincing slightly as he saw the obvious pain her tight squeeze inflicted on Haircut.

The doctor then moved along the line to Virgin and his semi-erect member. 'Now, that's more like it, Sergeant,' said the doctor as she grabbed hold of Virgin's rather large balls, sending his penis to full-blown erection.

'Stand at ease, soldier!' yelled Sergeant Fisher, watching Virgin's huge penis come to attention.

The doctor seemed to admire Virgin's manhood, whilst apparently sub-consciously massaging his balls with her right hand for a while, before coming back down to earth and moving on.

Next on the agenda was the eyesight test, which took forever, as each one of the recruits was asked to cover alternate eyes and read from the Snellen chart. The fact that they still had their trollies around their ankles allowed the doctor more time to admire each of their backsides. *She seems a right pervy slut!*

Feeling rather bored at this point and sick of the sight of bare teenaged asses, I decided to have a bit of fun with the doctor myself. Firstly, I carried out a commando test by flying up her very short skirt. I can confirm she was going commando. She was also wearing stockings and suspenders and was as bald as a coot.

If only I were human, I thought as I tickled the inside of her right thigh, making her wriggle like a snake charmer's charge as she tried and failed not to react to my little hairy legs teasing. She was soon diving back behind the temporary screen and scratching her thigh. She still had her hand up her skirt when the sergeant, thinking she had done with it, folded up the screen.

The potential recruits looked first at the doctor, then at Virgin, before bursting out in fits of laughter as they saw that his member was once again standing to attention.

Sad git, I thought as I once again dived up the doctor's skirt for another tickle.

Once the sergeant had regained control of the recruits, he promptly marched them over to the cookhouse for lunch.

Chapter Twelve
The BFT

After a rushed ten-minute NAAFI break, the group of recruits returned to the gym. Not for another medical; this time, they were there for the dreaded British Army's BFT. The BFT consisted of a three-mile run, the first half of which was run as a group in exactly fifteen minutes. The second one-and-a-half miles has to be run under the recruit's own steam and be completed in under eleven minutes.

They had only run less than a half mile when Haircut and Virgin and a few of the others started to fall behind. *Talk about being unfit. What chance do they have of passing the world-famous parachute training course?* I wondered as I sat on Bucket's shoulder, watching one of the PTIs giving Haircut a drumming down.

'Come on you effing bunch of fairies. What are you, men, or mice? Get a fucking move on!' shouted the PTI as he booted Virgin in the arse. The PTI was only a shorty, but his guns would have put a Chieftain tank to shame. He was someone you certainly wanted on your side in a fight.

After several kicks up the arse each, the run was finally over. Unfortunately, Virgin, Haircut, Fred and Teddy Edwards were amongst the eight of the twenty-two-man group that failed to achieve the eleven-minute target. They were informed that they would be given a final opportunity to complete the run again the following morning. *Poor buggers.* They were also told that failure to do so would end their military careers there and then.

Haircut and I will be getting on the train back to Crewe tomorrow, I told myself as I followed the recruits back to the accommodation block. There, they all showered and changed, before making their way to the to the cookhouse once more.

Chapter Thirteen

Testing Time

After what was another disappointing lunch, the group was once again frogmarched over to the main reception building, where several psychometric, basic maths, English and problem-solving tests awaited them.

The idea behind the tests was to give the recruits a choice of trades that best suited their skillset. Those with the highest scores would be offered more choices, such as the Intelligence Corps, RMP or Pay Corps. The others (the dumber ones) would be offered fewer choices, i.e. cannon-fodder roles in the Pioneer Corps or the Infantry.

I looked on as Haircut, Virgin and Fred seemed to struggle with the various tests. I saw Haircut scratch his head in confusion on quite a few occasions during the maths tests. *Maybe this is the end of the line for the trio?*

Once they had all completed the tests, the lads were marched to the NAAFI, where they were given an hour's free time whilst their tests were being marked.

Once they were sitting in the NAAFI, the lads started to talk about what particular choices they would like to be offered.

Virgin was the first to offer his wish. 'I want to join the Pay Corps; I've heard you can get quick promotion and you get to work in a nice warm office.' *Looking at how badly he'd done in the maths test, there was no way on earth that the army would put him in charge of the money. I've seen a ten-year-old do better,* I thought as I continued to chomp on the crumbs of one of the lads' Garibaldi biscuits that lay scattered across the table.

Next was Fred: 'I want to go into the SAS. I've heard they're the best fighters in the world!'

'You can't just sign up to the SAS, you have to have served as a regular soldier and then do a special selection course, you stupid fuckface,' one of the other lads outside of the now close group of three offered before laughing at Fred's naivety.

Haircut gave the intruder a stern look before slowly raising a single finger. The intruder starred back at Haircut, and the room went silent for a few minutes. It looked like a fight was about to break out any minute.

Yeah, I thought, taking my ringside seat on top of the salt cellar in readiness. Both boys were still staring at each other and slowly rose from their seats. The other guy was at least a foot taller and twice the weight of Haircut. I could see that Haircut's fists were clenched in readiness. They began to slowly walk towards one another; you could have cut the atmosphere with a knife.

Then the NAAFI door flew open; it was bloody Fisher.

'Right, you lot of bloody dumb-assed wasters, it's time for you to meet your fate. Outside in three ranks!' he yelled at the top of his voice.

Bastard, I was looking forward to seeing Haircut get wasted, I thought, somewhat reluctantly joining the group.

Chapter Fourteen

Three Choices

Once back in the main reception centre, the recruits were given a number between one and four. Haircut, Fred and Virgin were all given the number three and were told to move to another waiting area, whilst those with other numbers were sent to other various rooms.

The number ones were the smart group, and they would have the choice to join any of the Army's corps or regiments. The number twos could choose between the lower ranking corps and the Infantry. For the number threes, it was the Infantry or the Guards. The number fours were simply told they were not military material and were marched away to gather their belongings before being sent home.

Haircut, Fred and Virgin were the only ones to be given number threes. They then had three choices; join the Infantry, the Guards, or they could simply find their own way home. Being completely skint and not wanting to walk home, all three chose the Infantry.

Sergeant Fisher then gave them the list of regiments that were currently accepting new recruits. On the list was just one regiment: the Parachute Regiment.

'There has to be more than just the Paras,' Virgin protested.

Sergeant Fisher smiled at Virgin before getting up close in his face. 'You have three choices, sonny. One, the Paras; two, the Guards, for which you are too fucking short; or you can just fuck off. Your choice,' the sergeant offered. 'I'll be back in five minutes. I'll need your answers then,' said the sergeant as he made his way out of the building for a quick smoke.

'There is one good bit of news,' said Fred. The other two looked at him quizzically. 'At least we're all going to be training together,' clarified Fred.

'Yes, in a regiment that's renowned for having one of the toughest basic training courses in the world,' Virgin offered, using his fingers to emphasize "toughest". 'They'll make mincemeat out of us.'

'Speak for yourself,' said Haircut. 'I reckon I can do it. No problem,' he boasted.

Just then, Sergeant Fisher re-entered the room. 'So, is it three travel warrants home, or have you three finally found some bollocks?' he yelled, hands on his hips.

'We're in,' Haircut blurted out.

Fisher looked to Fred and Virgin for clarification. They both gave the sergeant a somewhat reluctant affirmative nod.

Now this I have to see, I thought to myself as I followed the sergeant out of the room and into the main admin office.

'You'll never believe this, but the three stooges out there have only gone and agreed to go into the Paras,' he said to the admin clerk, smiling like the Cheshire Cat.

'You should have given them a complete list of options, you sadistic twat,' said the clerk, holding up a piece of paper with a list of fifteen alternative regiments listed.

The crafty bastard.

'Nobody goes over the wall and shags my daughter and gets away with it,' replied the sergeant.

'Wait a minute, did they all shag her, then?'

'No, just Haircut. The others are just his besties.'

'How do you know for sure that he was shagging your daughter?' inquired the clerk.

'I saw him jumping out of her bedroom window this morning. That's how.'

Fifteen minutes later, Sergeant Fisher and I re-entered the room where Haircut, Fred and Virgin were waiting.

'Right lads, I just need you all to sign on the dotted line, and then you can take the rest of the afternoon off,' said Fisher, who was now talking to the lads as if they were old mates.

Each of them signed the relevant forms before being marched back in single file to their accommodation, where they would have to spend an extra night before attempting the BFT again the next day.

Having been ripped-off the night before, the three of them were now penniless and couldn't afford to jump the fence even if they wanted too. Which they didn't.

At five in the afternoon, me, the boys and the other five BFT failures all made their way to the cookhouse.

I hope the food will be better than the crappy slop they served up at lunchtime,' I thought, assuming my usual position on Haircut's back.

On entering the cookhouse, myself and the crew were once again offered slop, some of which had clearly been re-heated from lunch time. *I'll stick to the salad.* Once again, as I made my way to the salad bar I noticed more dead or dying comrades. Some of them had been there at lunchtime. *So much for clearing down between meals.*

Chapter Fifteen

Once More into the Breach

After eating, they all made their way to the NAAFI and were watching TV when Jumbo Jenny and a couple of her other portly friends walked in.

Virgin noticed them first. He elbowed Haircut. 'Here comes your bitch,' he said, nodding in the direction of the tubby trio.

'She's not my bitch,' said Haircut as he turned his back to them. It was too late, though, as Jumbo had already spotted him, and the trio made a beeline for them.

'Hey, Ben, how are you doing, honey?' she enquired as she pulled up a chair and sat next to him, placing her hand on his lap.

Haircut, being sober, was having none of it and promptly removed the offending hand.

Feeling a little put out with Haircut's lack of warmth toward her, she glared at him before introducing her companions.

'This is Juliet and that's Josephine. They're my sisters,' she said.

No shit! I thought to myself as I noticed the family resemblance of obesity, dark hair and butt-ugliness.

'How come you're still here?' asked Juliet, also pulling up a chair and sitting down next to Virgin.

'We failed the BFT, so we have to do it again in the morning,' replied Fred as he repositioned his chair away from Josephine, the third and ugliest of the trio. He was not interested.

Virgin, on the other hand, being the perv he is, and judging by the size of the bulge building in his pants, was loving Juliet's wandering hands.

'Are you not going into town tonight, then?' Jumbo asked Haircut.

'We're all broke; last night cost us a fortune.'

'Don't you mean cost Jimmy a fortune?' Fred interjected.

'Okay, it cost Jimmy a fortune. Fact is, we're still broke and Jimmy and his credit card have now gone home, so, no, we won't be hitting the town,' added Haircut.

'Well, if you're interested and willing to go into the NAAFI shop to buy us some booze, I'll pay. Then we can all go back to our house,' Jumbo offered, pointing at the other two girls.

The three lads looked to each other as they contemplated Jumbo's proposal.

'Hang on a minute, "your house", as in Sergeant Fisher's house?' asked Fred.

'Yes, our house,' Jumbo replied with a smug smile on her face.

'What about your mum and dad?' enquired Virgin.

'It's okay, he and my mum are at the sergeant's mess summer ball. They won't be back until at least five tomorrow morning.' Juliet replied reassuringly, whilst squeezing Virgin's thigh.

'I can't be bothered. I'd rather just stay here and watch TV,' mumbled Fred.

'I'm in,' said Virgin excitedly. Everyone looked toward Haircut in silence as he took his time to contemplate Jumbo's offer.

'Fuck it, I'm in too. Give me your money,' he said, holding his hand out.

Jumbo then delved into her bra and produced a rather warm and possibly sweaty twenty-pound note. Haircut tentatively took the money.

'What do you want me to buy?'

'Some lager and cider,' responded Jumbo.

'And some crisps,' added Josephine.

I then followed Haircut and Virgin to the NAAFI shop before joining the others and heading to Fisher's house.

Twenty minutes later, when Fred entered Sergeant Fisher's lounge, having unexpectedly changed his mind, he found Josephine pouring out the cider, Jumbo seeing to the music and Juliet busy trying to get into Virgin's trousers.

Jumbo, having selected the song from the 1982 film *An Officer and a Gentleman* "Love Lifts Us Up", sat next to a rather sheepish looking Haircut and placed her hand on his thigh.

Haircut, not wanting a repeat of last night's performance, once again removed the offending hand. It was at this point that Jumbo leaned forward to whisper something in Haircut's ear. *This I must hear,* I thought as I hovered in for a listen.

'Do you fancy carrying me off to my bedroom?'

'Not a chance, you're a bloody schoolgirl,' whispered Haircut, moving to the other end of the cream leather sofa.

Jumbo edged towards him again and whispered in his ear once more. 'I was a bloody schoolgirl yesterday, and if you don't take me upstairs and give me a good seeing to, I'll tell my dad and the cops all about your paedo antics last night,' she threatened, a smug smile on her fat face. Her attempt at blackmail was an instant success, as Haircut, now looking rather shellshocked, accepted her indecent proposal! Twenty seconds later, I watched on as Haircut was reluctantly led by the hand to Jumbo's bedroom.

I didn't blame him for giving in. It was probably better to give her what she wanted than to end up being banged up the arse buy some hairy-arsed convict on a daily basis – due to being jailed for paedophilia.

Still feeling a little queasy about the amount of Jumbo's flesh I had seen the previous night, I decided not to follow them on this occasion. Instead, I decided to check out the kitchen, where I hoped there might be some interesting scraps lying about.

Having not found any grub, I decided to go and see if Virgin was still in possession of his trousers. Then I noticed "Not Tonight" Josephine heading toward the kitchen. So, I spun around and followed her to the fridge, where she pulled out a block of cheese and started to hunt for a knife, leaving the fridge door wide open. I spotted a plate of dried up corned-beef hash on the middle shelf. Having never been able to pass up on corned-beef, I rocketed towards it.

I was enjoying getting stuck in when the light suddenly disappeared, and the inside of the fridge went pitch-black as the rotund Josephine slammed the bloody door shut.

Shit, shit, shit! I contemplated my incarceration and pending hypothermia, whilst still chomping on the hash. *God only knows how long it'll be until the fridge door is opened again.*

It was a good hour or so before Jumbo opened the fridge again and rudely stole my corned-beef hash. *Greedy bitch,* I thought as I made my escape. Normally, I would have punished her for robbing me of a corned-beef hash. Not tonight, though; I was just pleased to be free.

I made my way into the lounge to find that Haircut and his two sidekicks had already left.

Not wanting to spend any more time with the trio of corpulent bitches, I frantically zoomed around the house looking for an open window through which to escape.

Having not found a suitable exit, I resigned myself to being stuck there until Fisher and his wife returned some time during the early hours.

Eventually, at about five in the morning, the sergeant and his very pissed and amorous wife fell through the door and on to the floor, where they proceeded to rip each other's clothes off. *Not a pleasant sight.* It did, however, allow me to gain my freedom and reunite myself with Haircut and co.

Chapter Sixteen

By the Seat of Their Pants

I got back to the accommodation block just as the trio of hapless amigos were getting ready to go to the cookhouse for breakfast. Needless to say, I tagged along. Even though, thus far, the army slop-jockeys had not produced anything near edible, I thought I might try my luck with the remnants of someone's cereal bowl.

After eating their early morning slop, the three amigos and I made our way back to the accommodation block. There, we waited for Sergeant Fisher to collect us.

As I sat waiting, I contemplated what I might do if Haircut failed the BFT. *Do I go home with him or should I find another, more interesting donor of snacks?*

When Fisher turned up at 8 a.m., he was the usual gob shite. After reminding the lads that this was their last chance to pass the BFT and informing them of the consequences of failure, he marched them over to the gym.

Luckily for Haircut and me, all three of the lads passed the test by the seat of their pants.

I suppose you're now wondering why that was lucky for me. Well, this would be a bloody short story if Haircut hadn't.

Once they had been dismissed by the PTIs, Sergeant Fisher marched them back to the accommodation block, where they picked up their bedding and returned it to the stores.

As each of them exited the stores, the sergeant issued them with their train warrants. First to receive his warrant was Fred, who, by the time Haircut and Virgin exited, was busy protesting the lack of notice that he had been given regarding his posting. All three were not going home whilst awaiting the details of their course dates, as they had been led to believe they would. They had to report to Depot Para that very evening, as the course started the following day.

Upon hearing the news, both Haircut and Virgin joined in the protest. Which the sergeant ignored as he walked away, smiling to himself.

He's stitched them up good and proper, I said to myself as I prepared myself for what was yet to come.

Eventually, the boys accepted their fate, and together they packed their bags and made their way to the railway station, where we all boarded the first of two trains that would take us to Aldershot, known as "Home of the Parachute Regiment".

Chapter Seventeen
Welcome to Hell.

The journey on the first train that went from Birmingham to London was rather uneventful. The three stooges all sat together, all were silent and seemed to be in their own little worlds. They were probably contemplating what was in store for them.

Training for one of the most elite fighting regiments in the world would not be easy: compared to the Paras, Fisher was a pussy. I know this as I saw a documentary about it on my previous host's TV.

Feeling a little bored and rather peckish (nothing new there), I decided to check out the other passengers on the train. Then, suddenly, I heard the very familiar crinkling sound of tin foil being unwrapped. This usually meant someone was about to tuck into a homemade packed lunch. I traced the sound to an elderly couple sitting a couple of rows back. They were about to start in on my favourite — cheese and pickle on brown. *Bingo!* I temporarily ditched the trio of knob-heads and joined granny and grandad for elevenses.

I didn't go for the sandwich itself; I was happy to feed on the bits of grated cheese that fell from grandma's shaking hands and into the lap of her dress. It was safer that way.

By the time I was well and truly stuffed and making my way back to Dumb, Dumber, and Even Dumber, the train was pulling into Aldershot.

We all disembarked, along with approximately thirty or so other seventeen to eighteen-year-old boys. Who, I presumed, were in Aldershot for the same reason as my trio of idiots.

Once again, outside the station entrance, Haircut and co. were greeted by a sergeant and his coach driver. Both were sporting handlebar moustaches and monobrows. They were also built like brick shithouses.

Once again, the sergeant and the driver were very polite. Both wore one of those smiles that rather convincingly disguised their true feelings about having a new bunch of fresh meat to play with.

The journey to Depot Para only took about five minutes. As we drove through the gate, I noticed various groups of men; some were practicing marching on the drill square, others, wearing the now-familiar red, V-necked t-shirts, were exhaustedly running around the square and some guy was running around in circles while holding a well-polished tin dustbin over his head. All three groups had one thing in common; they were all being bawled at by either sergeants or corporals.

I looked toward my trio, and, not surprisingly, they all had the same look of fear and dread on their faces. *This should be fun*! The coach came to a standstill and the sergeant started to bellow orders at them in a way not dissimilar to the welcome they had received at the selection centre. Only this time, they were a lot scarier and the NCOs (non-commissioned officers) were a lot bigger.

Once the lads had disembarked from the coach, they were joined by the other recruits from the other coaches that had also rolled in. They were all ordered to assume the press-up position and push fifty. Needless to say, they all struggled. Haircut only managed seventeen before collapsing flat on his face. They were then ordered to lie on their backs with their legs raised six inches off the ground. Again, Haircut was the first to give up. This didn't go unnoticed by the sergeant, who made a beeline for Haircut. The sergeant placed his size thirteen boot on the small of Haircut's back.

'What's your name, dickhead? asked the sergeant as he applied enough pressure with his boot to squeeze the air out of Haircut.

'Ben Baxter, Serjeant,' winced Haircut.

'Why the fuck are you here son? Is it some sort of fucking joke? If it is, I'm not fucking laughing.'

'Uh, no, Sergeant.'

The sergeant removed his foot from Haircut's back. 'Stand up, dickhead,' he ordered, before getting up close in Haircut's face. After a few minutes of the sergeant staring directly at Haircut, he stepped back and cocked his head to the right a little. 'I see you've met Billy the Kid. What did you do to piss him off, dickhead?'

Haircut paused for a few seconds before attempting to reply. 'I…'

'You didn't take the piss out of his stammer, did you?' interrupted the sergeant. 'Have you got a problem with people with disabilities, Haircut? Would you take the piss out of my legless mother?' said the sergeant, who was now resting his forehead on Haircut's nose.

'No, Sergeant,' mumbled the now quivering Haircut.

Fucking bully, I thought, dive bombing the sergeant's ear and making him slap himself.

Once he'd had his five minutes of scaring the shit out of the recruits, the sergeant introduced himself and his team of corporals.

'My name is Sergeant Bucket, aka the Donkey. Do any of you want to hazard a guess as to why I have the nickname the Donkey?'

Bloody Bucket aka the Donkey. Really? More like Massive Dickhead. Why do you humans like to give each other nicknames? What is wrong with the one you were born with?

There were a few seconds of tense silence as the Donkey waited for someone to take the bait.

'Come on, gentlemen, I won't bite,' said Bucket, holding his hand up to his ear. Eventually, Haircut cautiously raised his hand.

'Yes, Haircut?' said Sergeant Donkey with a stupidly false smile on his face.

'Is it because you've got a big knob?' asked Haircut, bouncing back one of his own stupid smiles.

This sent some of the other recruits in fits of laughter, while me and the others became worried for Haircut's safety as Bucket's smile turned its self-upside down.

Donkey then once again got in Haircut's face. 'Are you a gay haircut? Have you been stood there looking at my crotch region wishing I had a cock as big as a donkey?'

'No, Sergeant, I was just trying to be funny,' replied Haircut, who was now shaking like a leaf and probably regretting speaking up.

'That's good to hear, Haircut. We don't like gays in the Paras; we eat them for supper on the way home from the Pegasus on a Friday night. We also don't like would-be comedians. I am nick-named the Donkey because I tend to kick dickheads like you in the bollocks,' said the sergeant, promptly kneeing Haircut in the balls.

Again, the reaction of the other recruits was mixed; some laughed uncomfortably, whilst others cringed in horror as Haircut flopped to the ground in agony holding his crown jewels.

Donkey then moved on to Virgin. 'What's your name, son?' he asked.

'Teddy Edwards, Sergeant,' replied Virgin.

'Teddy Edwards,' laughed Donkey. 'And where are you from Teddy?'

'I'm from Bexhill-on-Sea, Sergeant.'

'I know it well; the only thing that comes from Bexhill-on-Sea are gays, steers or queers. Which are you Teddy Edwards?' asked Donkey, getting up closer in Virgin's face.

'Neither of the above, Sergeant.'

'Well, you're not a steer, so you must be either gay or queer. I'll be keeping my eye on you, you fucking queer,' said the sergeant as he kneed Virgin in the balls, too.

Donkey then introduced Corporal "Killer" Kelly, a thickset guy who also sported a monobrow. His nose was so crooked it meandered down his face. You could tell he'd been involved in a fight or two in his time.

The other corporal went by the name of Corporal "Brains" Bailey. I somehow got the impression from the dumb and vacant expression on his ugly mug that his nickname was a piss-take that had stuck. He, too, was built like the proverbial brick shithouse.

Once the introductions were over, the recruits were separated into two groups. Each group was then allocated a corporal, whose job it was to babysit the recruits until they were either thrown out or passed out. Haircut's trio was allocated Corporal "Brains" Bailey. Who, from this point onwards, will be referred to as Brains, with Sergeant Bucket as Donkey. I can't be arsed to type their full titles every time they're mentioned.

Anyway, after the corporals set the tone for the next twenty-three weeks by beasting the crap out of the recruits for a good twenty minutes, Donkey and Brains marched the recruits to the quartermaster's stores.

Having nothing else to occupy me and wanting to be rid of boring Donkey, who was constantly trying the swat me, I went along.

The store was pretty similar that at Sutton Coalfield. However, the distribution point here was manned by four, very different guys. One of them, the one lobbing boots at the recruits as they moved along the line, had only one arm. The one next to him, a rather aged lance corporal, had a huge scar on the right side of his face that extended from his hairline down to the base of his jaw. The eye-patch that he wore partially covered some of the scars. *This guy looks as if he's well and truly been in the wars,* I thought to myself. From the looks of the spherical swelling on his opposite cheek, he seemed to be sucking on a rather large gobstopper. As Haircut approached him, the lance corporal stared back at Haircut. 'What are you staring at, shit-face?' he growled.

'Nothing, Corporal,' replied Haircut, still staring at the lance corporal's ugly mush.

'Is it the scar? Does it offend you? Or is it this?' said the lance corporal as he removed a glass eye from within his almost toothless mouth, showing it to Haircut before popping it back into his empty eye socket and laughing like a demented hyena. Haircut was unimpressed.

'Does the other one come out, too?' he asked.

'They call me Lance Corporal Cyclops, so what do you think, dickhead?' replied the one-eyed lance corporal as he chucked a rather full, cylindrical, green kitbag at Haircut, adding that he, Haircut, should now "fuck off." His words, not mine.

Grubby, foul-mouthed bastard,' I thought as I moved along the line, dodging the barrage of equipment that was being hurled at the recruits.

The other two, who were issuing the bedding and the tin helmets, seemed fairly normal, physically, at least. *They're probably just fucked up in the head,* I thought to myself, hitching a ride on Haircut's backpack and adding to his weight burden. Once back outside, we all waited for the rest of the wasters, before being frogmarched at break-neck speed to the recruits' new home for the next twenty-seven weeks – the Block.

Once outside the Block, Brains ordered the now knackered recruits to once again assume the press-up position and give him twenty. This time it was Virgin who had Brains Bailey's foot on his back.

It was at this point, having spent the last three days with the motley trio, I realised I was growing quite fond and protective of them. So, I decided to treat Brains Bailey to one of my "special flypasts", straight into his left and then his right nostril. These special flypasts were usually reserved for habitual fly-swatters who doggedly tried to splat me into oblivion.

After reading the last stanza or two, you're probably thinking *Why am I reading this, and why can't I put it down?* The answer is simple; you want to know whether Haircut makes it into the Paras and if I live long enough to see it. You'll just have to read on to find out.

Once he had finished having his fun with the recruits and was probably tired of me exacting revenge upon him, Brains finally dismissed them.

'Right then, you bunch of fucking morons. Get into the Block and find a bed space. I'll be back in twenty minutes, by which time I want your kit stowed away in your lockers, your beds made up and you lot dressed in your boots, black for shining, your green denims and a red T-shirt, PT for the use of. Dismissed.'

What? This guy has been in the military too bloody long.

Curious as to where Brains might be going for the next twenty or so minutes, I decided to follow him. You know what they say – a change is as good as a rest.

I followed Brains to the NAAFI. Upon entering, I saw that the NAAFI was divided into three main areas; there was the shop which sold everything from booze and alcohol to electronics, and the rest.

There was the corporal's mess, a bar dedicated to lance and full corporals. On the other side of the building was the other ranks' mess. Both were shit-holes, with sticky carpets and grungy, plastic condiment bottles in their respective dining areas.

The bar, which served both hot snacks and beverages during the day and the same snacks but with alcohol in the evenings, served both messes. It was staffed by a young, plump albino woman, who Brains referred to as "Snowflake". However, the name on the badge resting on her substantial left breast read "Charmain".

'Morning, Snowflake,' said Brains.

'Mornin', darlin', how ya doin'? What can I do for ya, sweet?' replied Snowflake, smiling as she leaned forward, resting her ample boobs on the bar and giving Brain an eyeful of cleavage.

Brains eyed the bazookas for a few seconds. 'I'll have a cheese toastie and a can of coke, please.'

'Anything else, honey?' Snowflake asked as she re-arranged her ample tits.

'No ta,' replied Brains, picking up his Coke and joining killer Kelly, who had already been subjected to the Snowflake flirt.

'That bloody woman never gives up,' complained Brains as he took a seat.

'Don't worry, you'll be safe for a few weeks; she's got a hundred recruits to get through from today,' replied Killer. And both men burst out laughing.

From this conversation, I could only presume that Snowflake was considered to be the camp bike. *I can't wait to see what she'll do to Haircut and can only imagine how Virgin's cock will respond to Snowflake's tits,* I laughed to myself as I scanned the mess for scraps.

At this point in the book, some of you readers might feel that my description of Charmain is somewhat sexist and discriminatory.

Tough!

Having had my fill of scraps and getting a bit tired with the assassination attempts, I followed Brains and Killer back to the accommodation block, where they were joined by Sergeant Donkey before they entered.

Chapter Eighteen

That's What Windows are For.

'**S**tand by your beds ready for inspection!' bellowed the excited Brains as the trio climbed the stairs. I flew on ahead; I didn't want to miss a thing. I had a feeling that this was going to be fun to watch.

As I entered the first room, I could see that Haircut and his two besties had managed to grab a bed space in the same dorm. *Good, that makes life easier for me,* I thought as I landed on one of the windowsills.

The good the bad and the ugly entered the room in complete silence. All three were trying to look mean but actually looked like idiots.

Donkey, flanked by the other two idiots, slowly walked from one bed space to another.

Lingering for a few seconds at each one, they gave each of the occupants the evils. When they came to Virgin's bed space, Donkey got up close in Virgin's face, staring at him for what seemed like ages but was probably only for a minute. He then gave his sidekicks the nod as he pulled a fifty-pence piece from his pocket.

Meanwhile, the two corporals began to open the large sash windows.

'In the army, we have a test that determines whether a bed has been made correctly or not. This is called "the coin test". One should be able to drop the coin from a height of approximately two feet above the bed, and the coin should bounce at least once. Do you think it's going to bounce on your bed, shitface?' he asked Virgin.

'Don't know, Sergeant,' mumbled the terrified Virgin.

'Well, let's see,' said the sergeant as he stepped up to Virgin's bed and dropped the coin. It simply flopped on the bed.

No sooner than the coin had landed, the two corporals started to throw Virgin's bedding, mattress and his actual bed out of one of one of the windows. Then they grabbed hold of Virgin.

'Stop! As it's his first offence, you don't need to chuck him out on this occasion,' said the sergeant. The corporals pretended to look disappointed at the Donkey's leniency.

So that's what windows are for.

Donkey then moved to the next recruit, who came across as a confident lad and seemed to have had some practice at making a military bed. I later learned that he went by the name of Richard Heed. Really? What sort of parent sets their kid up for a lifetime of ridicule at birth? I also learned that he had indeed gained some experience of military life. According to him, he had enlisted as a boy soldier at the age of sixteen and had attended the junior soldier's college in Harrogate. He was kicked out of the college for beating up one of the smaller cadets, who had the audacity to call him "Dickheed". Donkey dropped the coin on to Dickheed's bed, and, lo and behold, the coin bounced right off. The sergeant smiled and, once again, gave the corporals the nod. They, in turn, chucked Dickheed's bed and bedding through the window. 'I can't stand smartarses,' Donkey whispered in Dickheed's ear.

It was at this point that I noticed Haircut staring down at his bed. Knowing that he was only two recruits from having his bed thrown through a window and being a complete knobhead, Haircut then decided to take it upon himself to throw his bed and bedding through the nearest window.

Donkey, not happy at the thought that Haircut had potentially got one over him, got so far in Haircut's face that their noses were virtually touching.

'So, you're putting yourself up as the platoon joker, are you, sonny? Well, since you've thrown all your kit out of the window, there is only one thing left to chuck out,' said the sergeant, giving the corporals the nod once again.

The corporals grabbed Haircut and dangled him head-first out of the window.

'We'll see who's laughing tonight, when you will show you bed at 22.00 hours on the parade ground,' said Donkey, smiling menacingly. He then signalled for the corporals to haul the by now shit-scared Haircut back inside, before moving on to Fred, whose bed also went out of the window.

'All of those who have had their beds chucked will join our joker here on the parade ground at 22.00 hrs,' ordered Donkey, pointing at Haircut as he left the room.

Talk about being a dick, I thought as I watched Haircut quiver in fear and then surveyed the carnage on the ground below. *That was uncalled for.* Note to self; punish Donkey and co.

Once the sergeant and Corporal Killer had left the dorm, Corporal Brains ordered the recruits to change into their PE kit and form up outside, giving them five minutes to do so.

Uh-oh, PE kit sounds a bit ominous.

When all the recruits had formed up, Brains double-marched them to the gym, where several sadistic PT instructors were lined up. All were wearing white vests and all six of them were built like brick shithouses. Each one would have put the fear of god into Mike Tyson himself.

One of the PTI staff, a staff sergeant, then addressed the recruits.

'Good afternoon, gentleman, let me introduce myself and my team. I am Staff Sergeant Nightmare and my colleagues either side of me go by the name of Corporal Nightmare. Some of you bright sparks may have noticed that we all have the same surname. That is not because we are all related, we are just a group of sadistic bastards who love to beast the shit out of recruits. Hence, we are all your worst nightmare.'

Right, not too intimidating, then.

Next, Staff Sergeant Nightmare introduced them to the bell. The bell was there for anyone who wished to give up on becoming a para. All they had to do was ring the bell and they would be despatched from Depot Para before the sound of the bell had time to fade. He and his team of fellow nightmares then proceeded to beast the crap out of the recruits for the next ninety minutes. After that, they were then frogmarched to the most feared piece of apparatus in the British Army – the Trainasium.

Upon arrival at the Trainasium, Staff Sergeant Nightmare began introducing them to the para's aerial assault course. It stood some seventeen metres high and is one of the most feared assault courses in the British Army. It is designed to access a soldier's ability to overcome fear and follow orders at height. It is unique to the Parachute Regiment, according to the Staff Sergeant.

I have to say, it's size and height did look rather daunting even to me, and I'm a feckin' fly!

It was whilst watching the recruits being introduced to the assault course that I suddenly remembered that I and the recruits had missed lunch. They were stuck here, I wasn't. So, I decided to skip the introduction and headed for the NAAFI, hoping that I could get my feet on one of Snowflake's sticky buns.

Feet on one of Snowflake's sticky buns? I hear you asking yourself.

We flies taste with our feet. You see, this book is also educational.

When I got to the NAFFI, Snowflake was once again flashing her milky white boobs and chatting up Corporal Killer. Luckily for me, he had just purchased one of her sticky buns and, as she was so busy trying to arrange a shag for the night, she had inadvertently left the lid off the cake stand, a situation I was obliged to take advantage of.

Once again, I was so busy chomping my way through several varieties of bun, I didn't notice Snowflake pick up the glass domed cover, which she placed back on the stand, putting me in lockdown once again. At least this time I could see.

It was a good hour or so and the oxygen level was falling to critical by the time some spotty-faced kid bought one of Snowflake's sticky buns, and I was finally free again.

Now, gut-bustlingly full and in need of some fresh air, I exited the NAFFI and made my way back to the Trainasium, where Haircut and co. had just completed their introduction to the assault course. They all looked completely knackered and, to a man, were drenched in sweat. Some of them looked as if they might even die from exhaustion. Staff Sergeant Nightmare addressed them once more.

'Right then, you bunch of feckin' wasters, that was shit, and you are all going to have to get a lot more practice in. Now, does anyone want to ring the bell?' he asked. The group remained silent.

'I said, does anyone want to ring the feckin' bell?' he yelled, cupping his ear with his hand. The majority of the recruits yelled out 'No, Staff Sergeant!' The staff sergeant then walked up to one of the recruits and whispered in his ear. I flew nearer. 'Ring the feckin' bell, dickhead, or I'll kick the living daylights out of you, you feckin' waster.'

The two of them eyeballed each other for a few seconds, before the young lad walked over and rang the bell. The staff sergeant then moved on to another recruit and whispered in his ear, too. A few seconds later, that recruit also rang the dreaded bell. This went on until six of the forty-five men had been persuaded to ring the bell – ending their careers as paras. *Poor sods. How long it be before Haircut rings the bell,* I wondered as I watched the six failures being frogmarched away.

Then, Haircut and the rest of the remaining recruits were marched back to the accommodation block, where they had just about enough time to shower and change in time for their evening portions of army slop.

Being full to the brim and having no desire to visit the slop house, I decided to take advantage of the peace and quiet of the swat-free environment and settled down for a little nap.

Chapter Nineteen
Beds on Parade.

It was the too familiar gust of air that usually preceded either an object or a human hand that abruptly disturbed my sleep and sent me into launch mode. As I flew around the room getting my head together, the clock on the barrack room wall informed me that it was seven in the evening (Yes, I can tell the time too!). Corporal Brains stepped into the barrack room and informed the group that they were about to undergo a three-hour instruction on how to iron their uniforms. *Now that sounds like real fun. Not.* I took my front-row seat on the edge of Haircut's locker.

For the next two hours, Brains bored the crap out of the recruits, showing them how to iron their entire issued kit, including their army-issue green shreddies. He then spent another half-hour showing them how to display the kit in their lockers ready for inspection. Then, at 9.30 p.m., he let Haircut and the other four recruits that were due to show their beds on the parade ground go and prepare their beds.

I decided that this was something I couldn't miss. So, I followed the quartet outside. The four beds, mattresses and the accompanying bedding were all lined up and waiting for them in the centre of the parade ground. Dickhead was the first to finish; myself and the others watched in anticipation as he put his bedding to the coin test. It was like waiting for a droplet to fall from a tap. He let the coin fall. It bounced off the taut bedding and on to the floor. Dickhead smiled smugly at the others as he retrieved his penny coin.

A few minutes later, Haircut stood back and compared his bed to Dickheed's. He probably knew it was nowhere near as taut as Dickheed's. He asked Dickheed if he could use his penny to test his handy work.

'Get your own bloody coin,' came Dickheed's reply.

Haircut didn't seem very happy with Dickheed's attitude and started to walk toward him, probably to give him an attitude adjustment. However, his actions were curtailed when Donkey and Corporal Brains appeared on the square. 'Stand by your beds,' hollered Brains.

I looked across at Virgin, *Oh shit,* I thought as I saw that Haircut's bed was nowhere near ready for inspection. The sergeant and the corporal headed straight for Dickheed, and, as expected, the sergeant's coin bounced. He moved on to the next recruit, where the coin also bounced off the bed. The sergeant then moved on to Haircut's bed. The coin, as expected, simply flopped onto the saggy top blanket. 'Oh dear, it looks like we have a floppy, Corporal,' said the sergeant, a look of false disappointment on his face.

The sergeant looked across at Virgin's bed. 'No point in trying there, Corporal.'

'No, no point at all, Sergeant,' confirmed the corporal.

The sergeant turned to the recruits who had passed his coin test. 'You two help each other get your beds back in to the block.' He then turned to Haircut and Virgin. 'You two can sleep right here,' he said, before he and Brains walked off grinning like Cheshire Cats.

Now, correct me if I am wrong but that does seem a little inconsiderate. After all, how am I supposed to keep an eye on Haircut if he is stuck out here? I'm certainly not sleeping outdoors; it's bloody freezing in the early hours.

I decided to head back into the accommodation block and find me somewhere nice and warm for the night. However, the front door to the block was well and truly shut. Also, some bright sparks had shut all the windows. *Thank you very fucking much, guys!*

Having been locked out of the block, I decided to seek alternative accommodation elsewhere. During my search for a warm haven, I caught site of Snowflake outside the back of the NAAFI. She was kneeling in front of some guy, who, by the look of things, had just received a blow job from the lovely Snowflake.

Curious to know who was so desperate for a blowie they were willing to dip their member into Snowflake's ugly face, I flew a little closer. It was none other than the one-eyed lance corporal from the stores. Who, weirdly, seemed to be sucking on his glass eye while receiving head. *What's that about? Then again,* it m*akes sense – someone that butt-ugly probably couldn't get a blowie anywhere else,* I told myself as I watched the two of them set off in different directions.

Having looked for and failed to find a way into the NAAFI, I decided to return to Haircut and Virgin on the parade ground. As I approached, I could see that one of the recruits had company. As I flew closer, I could see Snowflake was sitting on the edge of Virgin's bed. The dirty bitch was actually giving Virgin a hand-job in the middle of the parade ground. *Has she no shame? I* could see from Virgin's quivering body that ejaculation was not far off – a sight I had no desire to see. So, I continued my search for an entry point into the NAAFI.

Chapter Twenty
Odd or Even?

Following an uncomfortably cold and wet night, Haircut and Virgin were allowed to move their beds back into the block. After a warm shower and a very welcome breakfast, Haircut and the other recruits were picked up by Brains and marched over to the drill square.

Upon arrival, Brains introduced the recruits to the drill sergeant. 'This is Sergeant Harding-Dempster. He will be your drill instructor throughout your training. You will see that Sergeant Harding-Dempster is carrying a pace stick. Some of the drill staff use this stick to measure their pace and the pace of recruits. However, …'

'That will do, Corporal,' the drill sergeant interrupted. 'I'll take it from here.' He waved the annoying corporal away.

'As the corporal was saying, my name is Sergeant Harding-Dempster. Some call me "the Corrector". However, you may refer to me as drill sergeant. He was also about to introduce you to my pace stick and the fact that I use it for other purposes. I call it my correction stick,' he said as he walked along the line of recruits, before stopping and flicking the stick into the balls of one of them, who went down like a sack of spuds. 'Hence the nickname the Corrector. Do you get my drift?' he bellowed.

'Yes, Drill Sergeant,' the recruits replied.

Why is it that all paras feel the need to have bloody stupid nick names? Is it to do with their size or lack of size of their of manhood? I wondered as I landed on his maroon beret, taking my front-row seat for what was about to occur.

The Corrector then ordered the recruits to form a single line, before issuing each of them a number, either a one or a two.

'Right then, listen up; when I give the command, I want the odd numbers to march one pace forward and the even numbers to march one pace back. Is that clear?'

'Yes, Drill Sergeant,' the recruits roared.

'Odd numbers one pace forward, even numbers one pace back, march,' ordered the Corrector.

All but one of them managed to follow his instruction. The Corrector approached the lone recruit. 'What's your name?' the drill sergeant asked menacingly, getting up close in the recruit's face.

'Private Smithe, Drill Sergeant,' the petrified ginger-headed recruit replied.

'Where are you from, Smith?'

'Liverpool, Drill Sergeant, and it's Smithe, Smith with an e.'

'There are only two types of people that come from Liverpool: scroungers and thieving bastards. Which one are you, Smith with an e?'

'Neither, Drill Sergeant'.

'You can't be a fucking Scouser, then. Tell me, why is it that you are stood all on your lonesome between these two ranks?'

'I didn't know what you meant, Drill Sergeant.'

'I gave you a number, either one or two. Which one did I give you?'

'Can't remember, Drill Sergeant.'

'Can't fucking remember? You really are a dumb bloody Scouser. What are you?'

'A dumb Scouser, Drill Sergeant,' replied the terrified recruit.

'Right. For the benefit of the stupid Scouser here, everyone form a single line again.'

The recruits formed a single line and the Corrector once again walked down the line giving them either a number one or two. When he got to Smith-with-an-e, he stopped. 'You stupid, are a number one. What number are you?'

'One, Drill Sergeant.'

'Okay, let's try again. Odd numbers one pace forward, even numbers one pace back. March!' screamed the drill sergeant.

I looked down the two rows of recruits. *Oh, shit,* I thought to myself as I noticed the Scouser Smithy had taken a step backwards rather than forwards.

The drill sergeant was now getting a little pissed off with Smith-with-an-e. He walked up to him and ordered him to stand at ease before flicking his pace stick into the recruit's balls.

'Are you trying to be funny, or are you really that fucking thick, you ginger-haired tosser?' Smith-with-an-e was too busy holding his painful balls to reply. 'I specifically remember giving you the number one. The number one is an odd number, you dick. What type of number is one?'

'An odd number, Drill Sergeant,' winced the recruit, still in agony.

The recruits were once again put into a single file and again given a number. Smith-with-an-e was once more given the number one. 'Let's try it one more time, shall we? Odd numbers one pace back, even numbers one pace forward, march.'

Smithy stepped forward.

Exasperated, the drill sergeant approached Smithy again. 'Either you are so thick that you can't tell the difference between odd and even numbers or you have a death wish. Which is it, fuck-face?'

'I genuinely don't understand what you mean, Drill Sergeant,' replied Smith-with-an-e.

The drill sergeant, realising he was on to a loser, simply told Smithy to step back two paces.

By the time the Corrector had managed to size them off, the drill lesson was over and Corporal Brains appeared back on the square.

'Can I have a word in your shell-like, Corporal?' asked the drill sergeant. *This I have to hear,* I thought, flying onto the epaulet of Brain's smock for a listen.

The drill sergeant suggested that the corporal arrange for Smithe to attend the education block one or two nights a week to brush up on his basic maths skills.

Brains then marched the recruits to the barber's shop. There, they were forced to have yet another haircut. Turns out the female barber was married to the RSM and would often be supplied with customers who didn't need a haircut, as well as some who were actually bald. Apparently, the money she made went towards her and the RSM's annual trip to Bora-Bora.

Chapter Twenty-One
First Pay Parade.

A month into training, the recruits where lined up for their first pay parade. In training, recruits are paid in cash on what is known as pay parade. Each recruit was due £480 pounds, £240 of which was placed into their savings accounts; £6 went to the RSM's wife for the haircut they never needed; £16 was collected by the kit insurance agent (the CO's wife); £12 was collected for the para benevolent fund, and, finally, £20 was collected by Smith-with-an-e for the platoon's end-of-training piss-up fund. *What bloody idiot thinks the piss-up fund will be safe in the hands of a Scouser?* I jumped on the back of Haircut's shirt as he and the others headed to the NAAFI. There, they were further fleeced to the tune of £45 for the unofficial uniform of bomber jacket and desert boots – the para's civilian dress code.

Reaching the four-week mark also earned the recruits the right to a weekend off. Some of them went home, whilst the others decided to hit the bright lights of London. Guess who were amongst the London crew? Yep, Haircut, Virgin, and their newest bessie-mate Smith-with-an-e formed one of groups that descended on London's Soho district that Saturday morning. I followed, of course.

Dressed in their green bomber jackets and obviously brand-new desert boots, the foursome disembarked the train at Waterloo and made their way to Soho. Little did they know that even wearing this outfit reduced their entertainment options, as lot of public houses refused entry to paras. The brand new and super clean desert boots also told unscrupulous club owners that the young trainees were fresh bait, just waiting to be ripped off.

Even though it was only eleven in the morning, some of the seedier establishments, those offering a free strip show, were open and more than happy to relieve the likes of Haircut and Co. of their remaining £141 of wages. However, the memory of their night out in Birmingham was still raw in the minds of Haircut, Fred and Virgin. So, he and his trio of friends decided to stick to the porn shops and public houses.

The first pub the foursome visited was the Intrepid Fox, a traditional Victorian public house. It was pretty much empty, apart from a couple of old tarts sitting in the far corner. They were dressed up to the nines and had probably just finished a night stint in either one of the seedy clubs or the many brothels that Soho has to offer. A quick look between their fishnet- stockinged legs confirmed they were going commando. *Probably street whores, then.*

The pub offered breakfast until 11.45 a.m. *Great, I've missed breakfast and I'm starving hungry. Hopefully, the food here is better than the crap the army slop-jockeys have been serving up over the last few weeks.* I hovered over the pub's hotplate, narrowly avoiding the spatula the tattooed punk-rocker chef tried to swat me with.

All the lads treated themselves to a £6 full English breakfast special, which consisted of two eggs, two rashers of bacon, two sausages, mushrooms, two slices of fried bread and with a pint of beer to wash it all down. I, on the other hand, helped myself to the to the free leftovers on the used plates dotted around the bar. It was far too dangerous at the hotplate.

Once the breakfasts had been demolished and the pints downed, the lads moved on to another pub, The Duke of Argyll, which was also deserted. However, by the time the boys sat down with their pints, a hen party of twenty women had walked in.

Problem was that they were all old enough to be the lads' grannies. Even though they were all well into their fifties, I noticed Virgin eyeing them up. *Fucking pervert.*

God know how long the hens had been out; they were all well and truly tipsy, and loud. Very loud. The bride, the one wearing an L-plate across her more than ample chest and with a big black inflatable penis strapped to her waist, couldn't resist waving at the boys, 'Any of you boys got one this big?' she asked mockingly. Nobody said anything, but the lads all stared at Virgin. After all, his cock wasn't that much shorter than the one the bride was waving. *If only those ladies knew.*

Ten minutes or so later, the hens started to play a game of hen truth or dare. One of the ladies chose a card from the deck. 'Truth or dare?' she asked.

'Dare,' the bride responded. The one holding the card proceeded to read out its contents.

'We dare you to passionately kiss the person to your immediate left.'

Without any hesitation, the bride tongue-kissed the red-haired hen on her left.

Another card was drawn. 'Truth or dare?'

'Dare,' said the bride.

'Find a man and sit on his lap whilst giving him a kiss.' *Uh-ho,* I thought as I saw the buxom bride-to-be head for Virgin.
Obviously, being the little perv he is, Virgin did not resist. And it didn't take much to get a rise out of his substantial member, which, I presume, the bride-to-be must have felt as she sat on his lap and snogged the face off him. 'Huge cock,' she shouted to her

other hens as she made her way back to her table, where the other hens quizzed her on the size of Virgin's manhood.

I looked across at Virgin, who was busy trying to hide his obvious erection. 'For fuck sake, Virgin, how can that possibly give you a hard-on?' Haircut complained, pointing to the bride-to-be. Virgin smiled, clearly somewhat embarrassed.

'I don't know about you lot, but I personally think we should get out of here before she get any more dares that involve doing anything with or to a man,' said Smith-with-an-e.

'I'll just go for a pee first,' said Virgin.

'More like a DIY hand-job,' said Haircut, taking the mickey and making the rest of the lads laugh.

A few minutes later, as Virgin was coming out of the toilet, one of hens called him over. *This I have to hear.* I took up my front row seat on one of the hen's flashing plastic cocks that adorned her Alice band, while the naive Virgin ventured into the pack of sex-mad cougars.

'My friend here tells me that you're hiding something rather large in your pants,' said one of the hens, stroking Virgin's inner thigh and causing Virgin's sizable manhood to inflate once more.

'Ooh, give us a look see,' said one of the other hens as she and the others surrounded Virgin and wrestled him to the bench seat, before trying to rip his trousers off.

Virgin just about managed to keep his pants on as he legged it out from the bar into the street, his trio of so-called friend in fits of laughter as he re-secured the belt that held up his trousers.

'That was bloody close,' said Virgin, sending the four into a fresh bout hysterics.

Having been to two, almost empty pubs and wishing to preserve their cash for later in the day, when they hoped Soho would live up to its name of London's number one entertainment district, the boys decided to do a little window shopping in the countless sex shops that dotted the streets of Soho.

Chapter Twenty-Two
Silky Sally

The tour of the sex shops was, for me, a real eye-opener. I didn't realise that the human race is so obsessed with sexual gratification. There were a wide variety of sex toys, everything from vibrating balls to dildoes of varying sizes, from tiny bullets to gigantic penises. And if role-play is your thing, they had plenty of uniforms for the ladies, from police-woman to a crotchless Wonder Woman outfit. You name it, they sold it.

Although watching the young recruits examining the various "marital aids", sometimes with a look of complete bewilderment upon their faces, was amusing, by five o'clock it was getting a little tedious. So, I was chuffed to bits when they concluded that they had seen enough, and, like me, they were hungry again. They decided to get a MacDonald's. *Now, that sounds like a dammed good idea,* I thought as I once more took my place on the back of Haircut's bomber jacket.

While chomping on their burgers, Smith-with-an-e noticed that Virgin was now in possession of a brown, paper-covered parcel.

'What have you got there, Virgin?' asked Smith-with-an-e, pointing at the parcel.

'Nothing really,' replied Virgin, clutching the brown-paper parcel.

'It's one of those blow-up dolls you spent so much time looking at, isn't it? You fucking little pervert,' mocked Haircut.

'Well, it is, but I bought it as a joke. I'm going to blow her up and hang her from the block's flagpole.'

'Yeah, a likely bloody story,' Jake said mockingly, pretending to be shagging someone.

'You do realise that the sex shops are open pretty much all night, don't you, Virgin?' enquired Haircut.

'And? Virgin hit back, clearly getting a little annoyed at the guys laughing at him.

'Well, by buying that,' he pointed at the parcel, 'you've only gone and advertised to the whole of Soho the fact that you're a sexual deviant,' said Haircut.

'Oh, yeah, I never thought about that.'

'Obviously,' said Smith-with-an-e, sending the foursome once more into uncontrollable laughter.

Bloody humans; they find the weirdest things funny.

Next, the lads took a tour of the strip of Soho's seediest bars, those with some bruiser of a bouncer manning the door, whose job it was to first coax punters in with the promise of a free sex show and then gently persuade them to pay the extortionate bills.

It wasn't long before one such bouncer spotted the dumb foursome walking toward him.

'Hello, lads, I take it from the way you're dressed that you're in the Para's. I'm ex-Para myself,' said the smiling highway robber as he rocked from foot to foot.

'What battalion?' Jake asked, not believing a word of it.

'Three Para, twenty-two years, man and boy,' said the bouncer. *Probably lying.*

'We've got a live sex show starting in a few minutes. It's usually a tenner entrance fee but because it's early and quiet at the moment, I'll let you in for free.'

'What's the catch?' asked Haircut suspiciously.

'No catch, I'll even give you a voucher for a free drink each because you're paras,' smiled the crooked bouncer, handing Haircut the free drinks vouchers.

'What's in the parcel?' the bouncer asked, pointing to Virgin's package.

'An inflatable,' replied Jake.

'Male or female?' the bouncer asked as he waved them down a set of steep stairs.

'Male!' shouted Haircut, sending the four of them into fresh laughter.

Did they learn nothing from their disastrous night out in the Midlands? I followed them down the steep stairs and into the almost-dark bar. The only light in the place was from a few scattered, red-bulbed pendant lights that hung above each of the seating booths, which surrounded a small stage. *The place screamed rip-off-dive.*

The lads approached the bar. 'What can I get you, boys?' asked the toothless old hag behind the bar, who thought nothing flashing her scrawny chest. Another sign the boys failed to notice.

'Four pints of lager, please,' replied Haircut, holding out his voucher.

'We only do cans. Take a seat, and I'll have one of the girls bring them over,' said the hag, taking the voucher with smile that revealed several gaps where teeth should have been.

While the boys selected a booth and waited for their drinks to arrive, I decided to explore the not-so-exotic establishment. I decided to take a look backstage first. There I found what was obviously the girls' dressing room. When I say girls, I really mean women's, as not one of the scantily clad females was under the age of forty. Neither were they good-looking. *Hence the need for the soft, almost non-existent lighting.* All of them were dressed in various types of lingerie, from fishnet-stocking and G-strings to boob-less teddies and were ugly enough to put you off your food.

Disappointed with the view, I decided to re-join the boys out front. There I saw two other scantily clad middle-aged tarts carrying two trays of drinks, one with four cans of lager on it and the other with what looked like glasses of orange squash.

I got back to the table just in time to hear Jake say, 'We didn't order any orange squash,' to the topless brunette.

'They're complimentary,' replied the waitress with a smile. Jake shrugged it off and asked what time the show was going to start. 'In a few minutes,' replied the other blonde waitress, before they both toddled off.

Ten minutes later, a few more suckers walked through the door. Most were young, like my bunch of idiots, and there were a few lonesome middle-aged mac wearers. All of them clutched a free drinks voucher. *Ex-paras, my arse. I knew that bouncer had been lying. It's a pity the lads hadn't caught on.*

Another ten minutes passed, and the boys were beginning to get a little impatient. They called over one of the now half-a-dozen waitresses.

'When is the live show going to start?' asked Virgin.

'They're just getting ready now, so it shouldn't be long. Would you like some of our ladies to keep you company while you wait?'

'Does it cost anything?' asked Jake suspiciously.

'No, their service is absolutely free,' replied the waitress, waving a couple of her colleagues over.

'This is Lola and Lexi. They'll be your hosts. Can I get you and the girls another drink, maybe the same again?' she asked. The four lads looked at each other before agreeing to more drinks.

A few minutes later, another waitress arrived with the drinks. Lager for the boys and what looked like flutes of champagne for their hostesses. *That's gonna hurt when it comes to paying,* I thought, dunking myself into one of the flutes, which turned out to be filled with cheap lemonade.

The hostesses wasted no time in downing their fake champers and getting cosy with the boys.

'What's in the parcel?' Lexi asked Virgin.

'It's an inflatable doll,' blurted out Smith-with-an-e.

'Male or female?' asked Lexi.

'Male,' shouted the other three lads.

'It's a female. Called Silky Sally, actually,' said Virgin, giving the others two fingers.

A few strokes on the knee and five minutes later, the girls were looking to the boys to top their drinks up. When the boys informed them that there would be no more drinks coming, the hostesses rapidly moved on to some odd sod who was sitting alone in the corner of the club.

Ten minutes later and sick of waiting for the "live sex show", the lads asked for the bill.

When the hag from the bar arrived with the aforementioned bill, the boys were once again not happy. It read as follows:

4 x complimentary Orange Drinks	Free
4 x Entrance fee	Free
8 x Lager	£80.00
2 x Champagne	£36.00
Suggested Gratuity 15%	£14.40
Total	**£130.00**

'I thought the first drink was free, so you should only be charging us for four lagers,' complained Haircut as he shared the astronomical bill with the others.

'The offer was for a free soft drink, which we gave you. You have to pay for alcoholic drinks,' replied the barmaid, with a look on her face that said she was in no mood to take any shit.

Knowing from experience that arguing with this type of establishment was pointless and could lead to a good kicking, the lads paid up and left.

That was the first and last titty bar the boys will be visiting tonight, I thought as I regurgitated on the barmaid's tuna sandwich before joining the lads outside.

Chapter Twenty-Three
Is She, or Isn't She?

Having been ripped off once again, and with their funds now running low, the foursome decided to do a little more window shopping before visiting a few more of Soho's normal pubs, which at nine in the evening were still pretty lifeless.

Just when the boys were about to give up on finding a decent place, they came across The Swiss Tavern. It wasn't exactly rocking but there was music and, more importantly for the boys, there were several groups of partygoers.

As the boys went to the bar, I decided to take a look around. I don't know why, but I had a feeling that the boys might be out of place. My suspicions were confirmed when I noticed two guys snogging the faces off each other in one corner and a couple of women grinning at each other in one of the booths. As I continued my tour, I got a distinct impression that the place was a gay bar. The pink-coloured cocktails most of the punters were sipping was also a bit of a clue.

I decided to have a taste of one of the cocktails that were sitting on the table of the two grinder-girls. I thought they'd be too busy to notice me landing on the pink ocean of alcohol. How wrong I was; I had hardly landed before one of them put a beer mat on top of the glass trapping me. *Bollocks.* I waited for the pair to observe me before they lifted the mat and set me free.

Having regained my freedom, I darted over to the bar where Haircut and co. were still waiting to be served.

If there was any doubt about it being a gay bar before, it was confirmed when the barmaid, who was dressed in a mini-skirt that barely covered her arse, turned out to be a transsexual, whose name, according to her/his badge, was Babs.

'Yes, sugar, what can I get for you, handsome?' asked Babs.

Haircut looked at the others for direction, then hesitated for a few seconds. 'Four pints of lager, please.'

'We don't do beer here, darling, only wine or cocktails,' replied Babs, now wearing a frown on their heavily made-up face.

'No beer! What sort of a pub doesn't sell beer?' blurted Virgin, looking genuinely confused.

'Take a look around love. It's a gay bar,' said Babs, waving a hand panoramically to emphasise the point. 'So, what will it be, wine or cocktails?'

Haircut looked to the others for advice. They all shook their heads.

'It's okay, we'll be off,' replied Haircut.

'That is a pity, you're quite cute,' said Babs, pointing at Jake and blowing him a kiss.

A few minutes later, the boys were once again walking the streets of Soho.

'I've had enough of this dump now. I say we cut our losses and get the train back to camp,' Jake said.

'We can't go back yet, it's far too early,' replied Virgin.

'Jake's right; this whole trip has been a disaster. Virgin nearly lost his pants to a bunch of middle-aged cougars, then we got ripped off once again in the titty bar and we've just tried buying a beer in a gay cocktail bar. Plus, the only one of us to get a woman today is Virgin. And she's made of bloody rubber. I say let's get the fuck out of here,' said Haircut, raising his hand as if registering his vote.

They all agreed that their outing to Soho had indeed been a disaster and voted to return to camp.

On the way back to Waterloo Station, the boys came across a scantily clad woman who was sitting on a window sill, smoking a cigarette.

'Do you reckon she's on the game?' asked Virgin, pointing at the woman.

'Probably,' replied Jake.

'How can you tell?' asked Virgin, curiously.

'Well, the only way to confirm it, is to ask her if she's got change for a thirty-pound-note,' replied Jake.

Virgin shrugged his shoulders, whilst giving Jake an "I don't get it look".

'It's simple, you ask her if she's got change for a thirty-pound-note. There's no such thing. So, if she is on the game, she'll say yes. If she's not, she'll tell you to fuck off,' explained Jake.

'Give it a go. We'll wait around the corner,' encouraged Smith-with-an-e.'

Now, this I had to see. I transferred from Haircut's bomber to Virgin's.

Once the lads had hidden behind the corner, Virgin approached the woman in the window. 'Excuse me, love, have you got change for a thirty-pound-note?' asked Virgin.

The woman looked confused. 'What did you say?' she asked.

'Have you got change for a thirty-pound-note?' he repeated.

The woman, still looking confused, called out 'Hey, Jack, there's some little fucker out here asking me if I'm on the game.'

Three seconds later, Virgin and I were being chased down the road by a rather large black man carrying a baseball bat. Luckily for Virgin, the over-weight husband gave up the chase fifty metres later.

The others caught up with Virgin and me a few minutes later, and we were once again making tracks to the station. Excuse the pun.

Chapter Twenty-Four
Naked Body on the Line

Once on board the train, the lads settled down with a few beers and a kebab each. *Great, I love the odd bit of kebab meat,* I thought to myself as I landed on a piece that had just fallen out of Smith-with-an-e's kebab.

Apart from the four of them and me, the carriage was empty. So, after they'd scoffed their kebabs, Haircut suggested that Virgin get his new best mate Silky Sally out for a look-see. At first, Virgin refused to release her. However, after a little persuasion from the others, he finally agreed to get her out.

Silky Sally was one hell of an ugly bitch. As Virgin ironed out her face, I thought she reminded me of an expression I had heard once. It went something like this: "If a lass had a fit body but was lacking in the looks department, she would be classed as a single-bagger. The idea being that you would only give her one if she wore a paper bag on her head during intercourse. Then there are the double-baggers. They're so ugly that you had to wear a bag, too, just in case hers fell off. Silky was definitely a double-bagger; I won't provide you with a detailed description of Silky Sally – I'll leave that to your imagination.

Also, I apologise to all the feminists that may be reading this. But it is unfortunately an expression that was used in the Para's in the 1980's. Plus, as I have said before, it's a piece of fiction. If you don't like it, you can always burn it with your bra.

Once Silky had been opened, they dared him to blow her up. Then, they took it in turns lean Silky out of the window at various stations they passed through. By the time it was Smith-with-an-e's turn, the train was about to pass through Woking, the second-to-last stop of the journey.

As Smith-with-an-e held Silky out of the window, an Intercity 125 shot past in the opposite direction, and poor old Silky Sally was sucked out of Smith-with-an-e's hand and onto the tracks.

Even though Virgin was a little pissed at losing his thirty-quid rubber lover, he too burst into a fit of laughter.

They had no idea of the consequences of their stupid prank; that is until the train rolled into Aldershot railway station. The platform was lined with a mix of civilian and regimental police officers, who promptly arrested them, taking Silky Sally's box as evidence.

Each of the foursome were placed in separate vehicles and driven to the Aldershot police station. I travelled on the cap of the copper who took Haircut.

Apparently, another train driver had mistaken Silky Sally for a real naked person, causing the whole of the northern side of the network to grind to a standstill, while the transport police recovered Silky Sally.

Once at the police station, the lads were locked up for the night, fed a rather scrummy breakfast, and well and truly reprimanded before being handed over to the Military Police. Who promptly sent them straight to the guard room, where the provost sergeant beasted them to within an inch of their lives.

The following day, they were hauled up in front of the commanding officer. He found them guilty of bringing the army into disrepute and fined them each £150 fine and seven days ROPs (restriction of privileges). Which meant no NAFFI, nightly kit inspections and absolutely no time to themselves.

Chapter Twenty-Five
Second Pay Parade

Eight weeks into training and the number of recruits waiting in line to be paid had gone from forty to thirty-one. Nine of them had either decided or been persuaded by the training staff that the army was not for them.

Unfortunately for me, Haircut was one of the nine. He was actually looking as if he might prove me wrong. His kit had not been lobbed through the window for a couple of weeks, and he was beginning to look like a soldier. So was Virgin.

Smith-with-an-e was first in line to receive his wages. This was so he could then join the rest of the highway robbers and collect the platoon's share of the end-of-training piss-up money.

The deductions were as before. However, for Haircut, Jake, Virgin and Smith-with-an-e there was an extra deduction of a hundred and fifty pound fine. Leaving the foursome with thirty-six pound between them to last the next four weeks. *I guess we'll not be going back the bright lights of London anytime soon.*

After the pay parade, Smith-with-an-e was once again dispatched to the bank to deposit the platoon piss-up money, which by my calculation now stood at £140, after the leavers were refunded their contributions.

I was a little bored with the camp and decided to join Smith-with-an-e on his banking run. I quite fancied having a look around Aldershot … "Home of the Para's."

The rest of the foursome made their way to the NAAFI television room. They didn't have enough money to do anything else.

Anyway, I hopped on to Smith-with-an-e's backpack, and off we went.

It was quite a tab to the town, and I was glad to be hitching a ride. The longer I stayed with Haircut and crew the fatter and more unfit I became. I have wondered on a couple of occasions whether my mission of proving Haircut didn't have what it takes to make it in the army was actually worthwhile. But the truth is, I had become fond of my gruesome foursome.

We eventually arrived at the bank. Having queued for about ten minutes, whilst several members of the counter staff sat twiddling their thumbs and pretended to be busy counting behind a sign saying "Position Closed", Smith-with-an-e finally reached the one window that was open for business. But, rather than depositing the £440, he instead withdrew the £800 he'd deposited four weeks earlier.

Now, that explains the packed rucksack. He's doing a bloody runner with the platoon cash. The bastard!

Money in hand, Smith-with-an-e then made his way to the railway station and boarded a train for London. I, on the other hand, had to try and find my own way back to camp, which took me forever.

Knackered from flying and dodging swatting hands, and starving hungry, I arrived back at the camp just in time to join the now trio for the evening serving of slop.

It wasn't until the following day that Haircut, Virgin and Jake noticed that Smith-with-an-e was absent. They thought he must have gone home for the weekend and thought nothing more of it.

However, as the others in the platoon also noticed Smith-with-an-e's absence, rumours that Smith-with-an-e had done a runner with the platoon's piss-up fund started to circulate.

By Monday morning, when Smith-with-an-e had still not shown his face, even Haircut began to suspect he'd done a runner. A little worried about his friend and his eighty quid, Haircut went to the Platoon HQ to report Smith-with an-e had not been seen since the pay parade on Friday.

By the time Haircut and I returned to the accommodation block, the rumours that Smith-with-e had gone AWOL with the troop piss-up fund were rife, and some of the others wanted his blood.

Their suspicions were confirmed two days later, when Smith-with-an-e was frogmarched in handcuffs to the guard room of Depot Para.

Twenty-four hours later, Haircut and the rest of the platoon were lined up on either side of the road from the guard room to the main gate. And, after going in front of the CO, Smith-with-an-e was unceremoniously frogmarched through the lines of recruits and up to the gate, where he was made to strip off his uniform before being booted up the arse by Donkey, as he exited through the gates and out of the army.

By the way, he was also relieved of his army issue shreddies.

Watching Smith-with-an-e scrabbling to get dressed and cover up his nudity, whilst being laughed at by the whole platoon was quite a sad sight. However, it was better than setting the rest of the platoon on him.

I think Haircut, Virgin and Jake were pretty gutted at Smith-with-an-e's departure. However, the trio did notice that Dickheed seemed well chuffed with the fact that four had now become three and, for the rest of the day, did nothing but go on about Smith-with-an-e's humiliating dismissal. Even though I was pleased he was now out of the equation (I was getting tired of typing Smith-with-an-e), I made a note to myself to punish Dickheed for what he had done to Smith-with-an-e.

Upon arriving back at the block to get changed for even more PE, Sergeant Donkey reassured the recruits that any money Smith-with-an-e had stolen would be replaced from company funds. He also chose Haircut as the new custodian of the piss-up fund.

Chapter Twenty-Six
A Whale of a Time

The recruits spent the next ten weeks carrying out build-up training. This training was to get them to a place where they would be ready to take on the dreaded Test Week at week twenty.

Build-up training consisted of a series of load-carrying marches and runs, circuit training, and military skills, like map reading, first aid, field craft and bayonet fighting, as well as weapons training.

It was during this period, on the weekend of week sixteen, that Virgin invited Haircut to his hometown of Bexhill-on-Sea. Of course, I followed. We set of for Virgin's house at about nine in the morning and arrived in Bexhill-on-Sea at mid-day. However, they didn't go straight to Virgin's house. They went instead to Virgin's local, The Traffer's Bar, where they both got extremely pissed. So pissed, in fact, that they became separated. I didn't know where Virgin had got to. But I do know what happened to Haircut; he was taken home by Kylie, aka the Beast of Bexhill, who took advantage of Haircut's inebriated state.

At midday the following day, when Haircut finally woke up, he was naked and lay next to the twenty-eight stone, butt-ugly Kylie. I could see the blood fade from his cheeks as he checked beneath the covers and found them both naked. He tried and failed to crawl out of bed without waking the whale of a woman.

'Hey, babe, how are you feeling this morning?' she asked as she sat up and leaned across to the bedside table for her fags, revealing her humongous arse.

Still in shock, Haircut muttered, 'I'm good thanks, I need to get to Teddy's, I'm supposed to be staying at his. Do you know where he lives?' he asked the whale, whose huge boobs made a slapping sound as they clashed when she turned over.

The whale informed him that she didn't have a clue where Virgin lived, but reassured him that Virgin would be in the pub by midday. She also promised to escort him to the pub; once he had bought her breakfast at the local café.

By the look on Haircut's face, he wasn't too happy to be seen in public with the Whale of Bexhill.

After treating the whale to a gut-buster full English and several cups of coffee, she escorted him to the pub.

Twenty minutes or so later, Virgin arrived with a couple of fairly fit lasses.

'Hey, Haircut, how's it going, where did you get to last night, was it fun?'

'Oh, yes, I had a whale of a time. I ended up waking up to that,' replied Haircut as he nodded his head in the direction of Kylie the Whale.

'I ended up waking up sandwiched between them two,' replied Virgin, with a look of fake disappointment on his face.

Having learned nothing from the day before, the two of them spent the rest of the day and night getting well and truly pissed. Again!

I stuck with Haircut, and yes, he did end up waking up next to the whale the following morning.

We never did get to visit Virgin's house.

Chapter Twenty-Seven
Test Week

Test week was finally here, and, amazingly, Haircut, Virgin and Fred had all made it. There were just eight tests to complete and pass before being awarded the famous maroon beret. It looked like I might have to eat my words, but I was sure Ben would fall at the first hurdle.

Throughout the next seven days, Haircut and co. would have to do a run of ten miles, complete the Trainasium, a log race, a two-mile march in under eighteen minutes and go head-to-head with another recruit in the boxing ring. It was certainly going to be a tough week.

During the test week, the platoon lost five more men. Two of them gave up on the log race and rang the bell, one failed to complete the Trainasium and the other two sustained injuries that ruled them out for a few weeks. They would have to pass-off with another platoon.

Unfortunately for me, Haircut managed to complete all tests to a satisfactory standard and would be on the pass-off parade a few days later. The decision as to whether the boys had done enough to earn their maroon berets wouldn't be made until pass-off day.

Having completed Test Week, there was only one thing left to do before pass-off – that was for the remaining twenty-five recruits, Donkey and Brains to spend the £2,660 platoon piss-up fund. And where did they go? Yes, that's right, the titty bars of SOHO. They started their pub/club crawl at six in the evening, and by ten most of the other recruits had used their common sense and returned to Aldershot. That left a group of six, which consisted of Haircut, Virgin, Fred, a very pissed Donkey, Brains and a stone-cold-sober Harding-Dempster.

The next bar they went into was a gay bar called The Admiral Dick. It was a very busy and very gay bar. It was the type of place where straight and gay people partied together and was actually rocking by eleven.

That was when a well and truly pissed Brains staggered up to the table where the rest of the group were sitting and introduced Geraldine, a not-so-convincing trans, whose real name was probably Bob. To the rest of the group and me, Geraldine's five o'clock shadow and her huge hands gave her away. The fact that she was also at least six-foot-three was also a bit of a clue.

Most of the guys were cool with Geraldine joining the group, after all, it was a gay bar. Then, at some point Brains realised that Geraldine was actually a Bob. Shocked and embarrassed at his discovery, Brains flipped, pushed her off his knee and onto the floor, while hurling homophobic abuse at her. This didn't go down well in a pub full of gays, and soon all hell broke out as Brains and the rest of the group were set upon by a few of Geraldine's gay body-builder friends.

By the time the group had escaped and reformed outside, they realised that Virgin was missing. They were about to send Fred back into the bar to look for him, when Virgin strolled around the corner.

'Hi, guys, what's happened to you lot?'

'Never mind that, where have you been?' asked Haircut.

'I got a bit hot, so I went for a little walk,' lied Virgin, trying to hide a carrier bag behind his legs.

Brains' nose had been rearranged somewhat, and it was decided by Donkey that he should escort Brains to the nearest A&E. Harding-Dempster, being the creep he was, went with Donkey and Brains, leaving the trio with the remaining £800 of the piss-up fund to spend.

Now that Haircut, Fred and Virgin were again on their own, they headed straight to the titty bars of Soho. There, they were once again ripped off. Only this time they didn't care. It wasn't their money. Plus, they were soon to be proper paras.

By the time the trio arrived back at camp at one in the morning, the rest of the platoon was fast asleep. So, we all retired for the night.

Their next few days were taken up with practicing the drill parade and getting their kit prepared for inspection.

In the early hours of pass-off day, at three in the morning to be precise, I was snoozing on Haircut's bedside table, when I was woken by the sound of Virgin getting dressed. *Where the hell is he going at this time of night?* I wondered as I followed him and his carrier bag to the roof of the regimental headquarters building. There, he inflated his replacement Silky Sally and attached her to the flagpole.

Chapter Twenty-Eight
Pass-Off

Pass-off had finally arrived. It was a bit of a sad day for me. Haircut and co. finally receiving their maroon berets also meant that Haircut had proven me wrong. Normally, I would hate being proven wrong. But on this occasion, and having seen what Haircut had achieved over the past twenty-odd weeks, I was quite happy to be proved wrong. Also, today would be the last day that I would take a ride on Haircut's back. Today we would part ways and probably never see each other again. I hate to admit it, but I had actually grown quite found of my trio of quirky amigos.

That's enough of that tosh. They are humans, and I'm a fly. Their sole purpose in life seemed to be to swat flies: Mine is to annoy the crap out of them.

The boys' final day started with a special breakfast at six in the morning. How was it special? I hear you asking. It was cooked by a civilian company of chefs, who were also preparing the visitor's pass-off lunch. *The army probably didn't want to risk giving the guests food poisoning.*

After breakfast, the platoon was tasked with laying out the chairs for their and the other platoons' numerous parents, girlfriends etcetera.

Then came one final dress-rehearsal before going back to the block to get changed into their parade uniforms. I have to say that all the recruits looked unrecognisable from when they first arrived at Depot Para. They seemed taller, broader and definitely smarter – dress-wise, at least.

Meanwhile, I joined the RSM (regimental sergeant major), who was accompanied by Corporal "Killer" Kelly as they inspected the parade ground ahead of the arrival of the coachloads of visiting parents that had come on the train and been picked up at the station. Killer seemed quite happy with the layout, nodding his head occasionally with approval. That is, until he looked up and saw a nude Silky Sally dangling from the HQ flagpole.

'Holy crap, Corporal! What the fuck is that doing up there?' barked the RSM, pointing toward the offending item.

'Shit, I'll go and sort it, sir,' replied Killer, legging it to the HQ building. Not wanting to miss seeing Killer manhandle Silky, I landed on the RSM's peaked-cap.

Killer eventually appeared in view on the roof of the HQ building and attempted to pull Silky down. However, Virgin had secured Silky firmly to the flag's drawstring, so Killer had to shimmy up the pole to release it. After a little struggle, the corporal eventually released the doll. However, on his way back down the pole he slipped and accidently let go of Sally. After Silky Sally had danced in the morning breeze for a while, she floated down and landed on the windshield of the visitor's coach, blocking the driver's visibility and forcing him to stop suddenly.

The parade was due to start at noon sharp. At ten minutes to, the camp commander addressed the recruits, who were now lined up around the back of the block.

'Recruits, you came here as boys and today you will walk out of this camp as men. Unfortunately, not all of you will be receiving the maroon beret today, but those that don't will be given another chance at Test Week in a few weeks' time. However, you trained together, and you will all pass-off together. Those…'

Boring, I thought to myself, opting to go and check out the parade ground and the people gathered there.

I noticed that the general, who was the commander of the pass-off, had an impressive number of medals. He had so many that I just had to take a closer look. While I was doing that that, I suddenly felt the crushing blow to the back of my head. The general had only gone and swatted me!

I guess there are some of you who might be thinking that the ending to this story leaves too many questions unanswered. Such as, did Ben get his maroon beret? And how the hell did I write this book in the past tense?

To find out, you'll just have to read Book Two – it's out soon!

The End

For now

Other Books by P T Saunders

Cupboard Boy
A shockingly true story of child abuse

Me and My Black Dog
A truly disturbing account of a Falklands/SAS veterans battle with PTSD and His eye-opening stay on a psychiatric ward.

Sleeping with PTSD
An anthology of PTSD nightmares and prose

I Saw
A soldier's emotive story of loss and his journey into PTSD

Left Behind
A gripping psychological thriller you won't be able to put down

&

Left Behind Two
Alex is Back
A chilling sequel to Left behind

Printed in Great Britain
by Amazon

14155562R00071